CUTHBERT
Nursing a Grudge

#8

by

Patrick Barrett

A Wild Wolf Publication

Published by Wild Wolf Publishing in 2016
Copyright © 2016 Patrick Barrett

ISBN: 978-1-907954-57-3
Also available as an e-book

www.wildwolfpublishing.com

Chapter One

Now and again the crow forced himself to leave the Valley before it eroded his reality completely.

He swerved the invisible motorways of the skies until he spotted a newly built complex beneath him. Two tall blocks had been built with hundreds of windows glittering in the sun.

The crow ended a graceful glide and flared into a landing next to another crow on top of one of the blocks.

Nudging the local bird with his wing, the Valley crow asked, "What's all this then?" nodding towards the next block.

The local crow rolled one beady eye towards his visitor and replied, "Look-out tower for us crows, innit?"

The Valley crow studied the huge complex and discovered another design flaw in his makeup; he had no eyebrows, so he couldn't raise one quizzically at this statement. "The humans built these huge towers just so crows could look for food?"

"'Course," replied the local crow, "Why else would they do it?" He then stabbed his beak under his wing-pit and searched for a snack.

The Valley crow braced himself against a gust of wind and observed, "But that one is full of people - what makes you think it's a watch-tower?"

The local crow emerged disappointed from under his wing-, sighed and answered slowly and deliberately, "Because I'm on top and I'm watching, that's why. Not from around here, are you mate?"

The Valley crow, still studying the opposite block, waved one wing vaguely. "No, from the valley over there."

The local crow's eyes widened. It was impossible for a coal-black crow to turn pale, but the skin between his feathers puckered until his quills rattled. He began to side-step away from his visitor until he simply fell off the edge, hoping for a gale-force escape route.

He had heard about the Valley, everyone had - nothing going in came out the same, if it ever came out at all.

With a stiff breeze safely tucked under his wings, he made his escape.

The Valley crow sensed he was alone and shrugged. *Just another out of the Valley experience,* he thought.

Studying the building intently, he cocked his head from side to side. This had the effect of rattling all his thoughts into the middle to form a conclusion.

"Hah!" he squawked.

Behind every window was a bed with a human in it and other humans scuttled in and out attending to their needs.

He had seen something like this before. Nodding to himself, he remembered an old flightless crow known as 'cloud-hopper' knocking a beehive over. It was that day all over again, except for the squadrons of lunatic, kamikaze bees, of course. All these humans must be special and the drones were looking after them, just like the bees.

The Valley crow stretched his feathers luxuriously before taking off to look for the giant honeycomb.

Chapter Two

The Valley was experiencing a period of boredom. Every so often life began to seem routine and a collective thought emerged.

Let's do something different.

The bar at the Mandrake Arms was crowded and everyone had an idea for Cuthbert to act upon.

In the corner Henry and the Captain discussed Julius Caesar and his reasons for crossing the Rubicon.

"He had to make a point," said the Captain. "It was a show of force to prove his legions were behind him and make the senate pay attention."

"But it was illegal for Roman troops to cross the boundary of the Rubicon river," said Henry. "He was risking everything."

They were so engrossed in the discussion that the stealthy slap of Percy's turned down wellies wasn't heard as he crept through the throng and appeared at Henry's shoulder.

He sighed loudly before announcing, "You lot with your education and your books; you always miss the obvious, don't you?"

Henry and the Captain stiffened. The adrenaline was flowing and it drowned out the squeaks of common sense that normally protected them from Percy.

"All right then, Percy," snapped the Captain, "what was Caesar's overwhelming desire to cross the Rubicon based on?"

He almost fell off his chair as Percy replied, "Gardening."

"Gardening?" spluttered the Captain, finding absolutely no assistance in Henry's shocked expression.

Percy supped at his pint before answering, "Of course, gentlemen, gardening."

The Captain's face was turning into a colour chart as he insisted, "He was trying to intimidate the Roman senate, he had his legions with him - why the blazes would he think about gardening?"

Percy sighed dramatically and sipped his pint again before announcing, "Every gardener knows that all the best vegetables grow on one side of a river, so what's the point of cooking for all those men without the best vegetables? That's why he crossed the river."

Henry shrugged as the Captain glanced despairingly at him. He took a deep breath, stared at Percy and said, "He was threatening Rome itself, he was risking civil war, his life and his career; why would he bother about food at a time like that?"

Percy sipped once more before saying, "That was his big mistake see? Always feed the troops and never skimp on the quality. Never make a good Caesar salad without the best vegetables, you know, mate." And he wandered off.

At the next table Cuthbert tried to appear interested as his mind played leap-frog from one excuse to the other. Suggestions came thick and fast and pretty much represented the people making them. He turned as Percy appeared beside him.

Percy studied the list in front of his friend and read the notations after each one.

Medieval Fair (Valley Mafia pick-pocketing extravaganza)

Shooting range (Ronald needing to shift some dodgy ammunition)

Hang-Gliding (Elspeth trying to get the bachelors to air their sheets)

Percy coughed to attract attention before suggesting, "Why not do another play by Shakespeare?"

Cuthbert brightened immediately. "Great. Which one, Percy?"

Percy was puzzled. "William, of course" he said.

Margery stood behind the bar cleaning a glass and chatting to the women.

Someone brought up the subject of ghosts and she had entertained everyone with "No-one has ever spotted a ghost around here. With all the men creaking and groaning no one would notice it."

Their laughter hid the approach of wellies and Percy coughed politely before asking, "Didn't you hear about the ghost of Fido when you bought the pub then?"

The laughter stayed trapped behind the lipstick as the women glanced suspiciously at each other before shaking their heads.

Percy hopped onto a bar stool and shuffled to get comfortable, beaming as Margery slid a pint his way. "Fido was born right over there by the fireplace," Percy began. "The locals adored him and sometimes he accompanied them home if alcohol-induced, blurred-vision syndrome occurred."

He sipped his pint, but no-one seemed impressed by his technical jargon, so he continued. "As he grew older, Fido became the guard dog to beat them all. He rescued lost travellers in snow drifts and fought off packs of scavenging wolves."

Percy set his glass down on the bar and leaned forward conspiratorially, and the women leaned in to show their interest.

"One night, the wolves came right to the Mandrake Arms and forced the door open; Fido fought them off single-handed."

The women sighed.

"After fighting them tooth and nail in the doorway, Fido swung round and kicked the door shut with his back legs. *BANG*." Percy clapped his hands together.

The women jumped.

Percy shook his head sadly. "His tail was chopped clean off."

The women sighed again.

"What happened then?" someone asked foolishly.

Percy picked up his pint again and it was his turn to sigh. "Poor Fido, he died of his wounds and the landlord fastened the tail over the bar as a monument."

Handkerchiefs fluttered as the women glanced upwards towards a vacant spot on the old beam.

"Where is it now?" asked someone, dabbing at a tear.

Percy leant forward again. "Well, when Fido reached the Pearly Gates, Saint Peter wouldn't let him in because he wasn't complete and he sent him back down to fetch it. Fido was disappointed of course, but you can imagine his joy at seeing his old master again and the fuss everyone would make of him at the bar."

The handkerchiefs really went to work now as emotion erased all references to a 'doggy heaven'.

"The landlord heard barking and came down in his nightshirt, only to find the ghost of Fido trying to wag his missing tail at him."

"What did he say, what did he say?" chanted the women in unison.

Percy paused for a moment and said, "Aw, come on, Fido, you know I can't serve spirits after hours." And Percy wandered away.

"Does someone *pay* him to do that?" growled Margery through gritted teeth.

Chapter Three

Cuthbert awoke early and set off for the village. The butterflies flitted past him and the bees hummed, so Cuthbert hummed along with them.

Someone once mentioned that all the creatures of nature had perfect pitch, which was a surprise to him because the 'Perfect Pitch Award' at school was always awarded to anyone who could hit Cuthbert on the back of the head as he walked through the school gates.

It didn't matter who pitched what or when, the winner was always Cedric. The boy was a marvel, he could hit a moving Cuthbert at twenty paces; he even made a cow-pat seem aerodynamic.

Always the school swot, Cedric became interested in religion and after being ordained he was briefly the vicar in the Valley.

He still managed to hit Cuthbert when he walked down the aisle swinging his censer at funerals.

His dedication to the religions of the world became rather confused as he grew older and the services were a hotchpotch of Anglican hymns, Catholic hats and Voodoo chanting.

When he finally passed away in frustration over trying to teach a chicken Latin so that it could make the responses as he sacrificed it, Cuthbert finally had his revenge.

Being the Valley's undertaker had its perks. He made sure the vicar was buried under a dung-heap, upside down, not facing Mecca and nowhere near the Ganges. Wiping his spade afterwards, Cuthbert considered the location.

"Looks like the perfect pitch to me," he muttered.

Cuthbert arrived just after Mrs Biggle opened the Post Office and stood, patient and alone, whilst she pottered around behind the mesh screen.

Glancing up, she scowled. "I hope you haven't pushed to the front again, Cuthbert. I'm keeping an eye on you."

Looking around at the empty room, Cuthbert sighed and continued his vigil at the altar of the twin saints Lick-it and Post-it.

Henry and the Captain came in behind him and everyone exchanged greetings as the Post Office gradually filled.

Mrs Biggle heard the murmur of customers and glanced up, again with a scowl. "You're at the front again, Cuthbert. I've got you down as a serial offender, you know."

The crowd behind him tutted obediently, just to get into the spirit of things and because it was always fun to watch Cuthbert squirm.

A commotion at the back distracted everyone. A voice called out, "Excuse me, coming through. Mind yer backs, there's urgent postal business, thank you."

A dishevelled figure swept past Cuthbert and demanded ten first class stamps, four chocolate bars and a roll of parcel tape.

Mrs Biggle snapped into action and quickly supplied the items and the visitor swept out with a cheery, "Thank you, Post Mistress, next one in line will pay."

Cuthbert gawped at Mrs Biggle. "You let him push to the front and then served him."

Mrs Biggle glared back. "It was urgent postal business, you heard him; he was an official postal worker."

Cuthbert spluttered, "*It was Percy with his hat on backwards!*"

The crowd collectively sucked in its breath and took a pace back.

Mrs Biggle maintained eye contact with the offender as she had been taught in the postal workers' self-defence class and slowly reached for her mobile phone. Without taking her eyes of him, Mrs Biggle snapped open the phone and yelled for help. Unfortunately, as usual it was her powder compact, and Cuthbert disappeared in a cloud of 'Kiss in a Mist' or 'Snog in a Fog' as the locals had dubbed it.

Cuthbert finished rinsing himself in the horse trough outside the Mandrake Arms and sat in the sun to dry.

The village had woken up and people collected in groups chatting amiably.

Percy grinned as he sat beside Cuthbert. "Never got the hang of queuing myself."

Cuthbert ignored him. There seemed to be a special set of rules in this life for Cuthbert and none whatsoever for Percy.

"Oh, nearly forgot, mate," chirped Percy, ferreting in his welly. "You had a letter."

Cuthbert gingerly accepted the screwed up offering and tried to ignore where it had been. The glue had surrendered to the pungent aroma of Percy's footwear and Cuthbert checked the contents. "Oh no," he gasped, "It can't be that time again already, it can't be." Cuthbert didn't understand fear - all he knew was that occasionally his brain took over all his responses and made him run.

Percy took the letter from him and asked, "Who's Nurse Brenda then?"

Cuthbert couldn't reply. The street had become deathly quiet and a dust cloud approached.

Avril went into work early. As the reporter for the local paper, she was duty bound to be on hand when anything dramatic occurred. A disturbed night convinced her there was something in the wind and she must be prepared.

After opening the blind over the huge window overlooking the street, she sharpened her pencil and dusted the computer terminal that waited in vain for electricity. The street scene was quite normal, but Avril did not relax.

A Pulitzer Prize will never come if you don't tell them where to send it, she thought.

Cuthbert straightened and stepped into the street. The groups of citizens gasped and stepped back against the buildings, looking first one way down the street and then the other as Cuthbert began to walk down the middle of the road like a man prepared to meet his destiny.

"Ooh, just like Gary Cooper in High Noon," gasped someone.

"No, gunfight at the OK corral," said someone else.

"Dozy Cuthbert trying to get run over more like," sneered Ronald.

Avril straightened in her chair. *What's Cuthbert up to?* she wondered just as a string snapped and the window blind came crashing down like a giant eyelid announcing sleep.

"Damn," she said and began to wrestle with the offending blind. She couldn't lift it in the middle and if she lifted one end, the other simply sagged again.

Spotting another dangling length of cord, Avril gave it a hefty pull. A mechanism somewhere activated and she was pulled off her feet until her fingers were wrapped around the top roller, leaving her suspended four feet in the air with no outside view whatsoever.

Percy sensed the urgency of the moment and, pulling out a pair of secateurs, shouted, "Here, mate, you might need these!"

Cuthbert caught them neatly and, squinting against the early morning sun, he continued his walk with the cutters gripped in his right pocket.

The dust cloud had rolled off to one side, and now a figure could be seen advancing down the middle of the street towards Cuthbert.

The crowd turned towards a steady 'chink, chink' noise as the secateurs rubbed against the loose change in Cuthbert's pocket. Then the crowd looked the opposite way towards the 'Squeak, squeak' of a bicycle wheel.

'Squeak, squeak' advanced towards 'Chink chink' and the atmosphere was tense. The two protagonists stopped about eight feet apart and Cuthbert rolled his shoulders and loosened the secateurs in readiness.

"Nurse Brenda," he drawled.

"Cuthbert," she replied flatly.

"I thought we agreed that this town wasn't big enough for both of us," hissed Cuthbert.

"No, Cuthbert, *you* agreed. *I* told you to belt up. Now, get out of the way and take your mangy Muppet with you."

"Oi!" said Percy from behind Cuthbert.

Cuthbert narrowed his eyes in true gunfighter tradition and studied Nurse Brenda. She hadn't changed, the dark blue uniform, the squeaky bicycle, the hair tied in a bun with at least three syringes stuck in it for easy access and the Gladstone bag full of nightmarish devices and potions.

"You tried to murder me," whispered Cuthbert.

Percy appeared alarmed. Was this some serial killer - should he run very fast and pretend to get help?

Nurse Brenda sighed. "It was a measles injection, Cuthbert, and you were fourteen years old. Everyone else had theirs at eight."

Cuthbert paled, his hand went for his secateurs.

Nurse Brenda was quicker and the syringe was in her hand.

The sun caught the needle in a flash of painful memories ... and Cuthbert fainted.

Percy looked at his fallen friend in astonishment. It was the only time he had seen him try to assert himself.

He quickly lifted his hat and slicked his unruly red hair down. "I'm Percy," he announced brightly.

"No, you are not," barked Nurse Brenda, "You are a flea-ridden, unhygienic apology for a human being and you will attend my clinic as soon as I have rounded up the Valley mafia."

With that she headed for the Mandrake Arms.

Avril freed her fingers one by one as she swung backwards and forwards inside her office, until she dropped free with a thump and heard a round of applause from the people watching outside.

In the distance she saw Percy's hat moving slowly as if he dragged something, but by the time the crowd had dispersed, the street was empty again.

Drat, she thought. *At least I'm looking forward to covering my first sheep-shearing competition.*

She had been dying to see how the sheep managed to hold the clippers with their feet.

Chapter Four

The kettle crashed down onto the stovetop and the range grumbled menacingly in retaliation. The teapot rattled like chattering teeth as the contents were swirled around and the cups were skimmed across the table.

Percy ventured, "Still upset, are we?"

Cuthbert glared. "That woman has humiliated me every time she appears," he snapped. "She was the mid-wife, the nit-nurse, and she was called in every time someone became mysteriously spotty."

By the time a spoon reached Percy, it looked like a magician's prop. He stuck it into a gap in the old farmhouse table and straightened it.

"I thought you were good at getting revenge," he said.

Cuthbert produced an evil grin. "No one better than me, Percy, no one better." He paused. "'Course they have to be dead first, so they don't really know about it."

Jasper paced in front of his troops. As the leader of the Valley mafia he was expected to have all the answers, and thus a roomful of eyeballs followed him. Jasper shivered, it was like staring into a pond full of frog-spawn.

He addressed his men. "We are facing the direst threat yet, gentlemen; Nurse Brenda is in the Valley."

Jasper paused as the gasps of horror and the question "Who?" built up to a crescendo, and he held up both hands.

"We are not going to be intimidated by a district nurse on a bike, gentlemen. The days of injections, nit-combs and funny coloured soap are over. Assemble here tomorrow with individual disguises, fishing line and any plastic explosives left over from bonfire night. Until tomorrow, gentlemen ..."

He watched them file out and chewed his thumbnail. Even the twins had never faced Nurse Brenda or, if they had, it was never discussed.

Chapter Five

The Mandrake Arms became an impromptu clinic. The ladies wandered in, had coffee, discussed 'laugh-lines' and rare blood and giving birth, before accepting a leaflet and going home.

Arkle had been busy in the fields filing a cow's hooves, but she simply dragged it behind her and consulted through a window in the bar.

The corner behind the curtain reserved for the men was empty and the pile of leaflets was intact. The approach road showed no signs of a male pilgrimage forming up and travelling together and the athlete's foot powder hadn't been touched.

Nurse Brenda tapped a gentle tattoo on the table top. "Okay, boys, let the games begin."

Jasper studied the lie of the land. His 'men' were strategically placed in folds and dips, and fishing line crossed the main path waiting to be pulled taut.

The Valley mafia had pooled their resources and produced some excellent camouflage, except for a scraggy-looking sheep that really gave the game away.

Impervious to the shouted insults, rocks and attempts to find out who he was, the sheep bit the nearest of his tormentors and rejoined his flock.

Nurse Brenda slid extra syringes into her bun and closed her mobile phone. She smiled and stepped out of the Mandrake Arms; she loved it when a plan came together.

Percy sat on a bench outside the pub swinging his little legs and watching the fumes coming from inside his wellies. For a moment, he wondered whether there was a church vacancy for an incense spreader, but then Nurse Brenda appeared.

Nurse Brenda took in the huge grin and the hat seeming to float above an explosion of red hair and almost recoiled at the ripe scent of old wellies.

"Don't worry," she said, "I'll get around to you. They're filling the sheep-dip as we speak."

Percy was content to grin and watch. He soon forgot to swing his legs as Nurse Brenda prepared for battle.

She unpacked the saddle bags on each side of her bike and laid an impressive array of utensils out. A telescopic intravenous drip stand was quickly bandaged to the handlebars and stretched upwards.

"That takes care of the fishing line," she muttered before fastening a huge pair of scissors to the frame at the front of the bike.

Then she mounted her machine and set off with a rhythmic squeak.

Percy ran all the way to Cuthbert's. He knew when something was worth watching and this was a mafia ambush.

Cuthbert had mislaid a corpse again, but not a different one to the last one lost. This was one he managed to mislay on a regular basis. He'd been a slippery chap when it came to paying for anything when he was alive; death just didn't change some people.

Percy burst in; slamming the missing corpse into the wall and causing the door to come straight back and knock him outside again.

"More haste, less speed," he muttered, rubbing his nose. This time, he crept up to the door and gave it one savage kick, which produced exactly the same result.

Picking himself up, Percy shouted, "Cuthbert, the Valley mafia are ambushing Nurse Brenda. Got any popcorn?"

Cuthbert and Percy settled down near to the top of the hill. They were soon joined by Henry and the Captain, both sensing entertainment nearby.

"Got to hand it to the little blighters, you know; damn good camouflage."

"Except for that pathetic excuse for a sheep," said Ronald, down beside them. "Jasper must be losing his touch."

Cuthbert watching Percy pluck a piece of vegetation and nibble at it contentedly. "Don't eat that Percy," he said. "You don't know where it's been."

Percy gave his friend a pitying look before replying, "I know exactly where it's been, mate. My gardening expertise allows me to live off the land in times of need," and he nibbled away happily.

"When did you ever live off the land?" sneered Ronald. This was the same man who tried to put the 'Merc' in mercenary, but ended up with a Ford Mondeo.

Percy pulled out another clump, shuffled, and replied, "There were times when money was so tight I was reduced to borrowing from friends, even when all they had left was spices, mate." He munched another handful and added, "Yes, I was living on borrowed Thyme for a while."

His companions groaned and Henry asked Cuthbert, "Was there a thistle in that last handful?"

Cuthbert nodded gleefully and watched the colour change on the back of Percy's neck.

They could see Jasper scuttling from one position to another briefing his men, then they heard the squeak.

Nurse Brenda scanned the approaching terrain as she began to pedal faster. Heads bobbed in and out of view on both sides as she accelerated into the narrow roadway winding through the hills, Ride of the Valkyries hissing between her clenched teeth in time with her squeaky wheel.

Cuthbert straightened as he saw her advance; this was heroism of the highest order. "This is just like that charge of the something's into the Valley of somewhere else," he said, pulling on Percy's sleeve.

"Spartans?" suggested Percy.

"No!" said Cuthbert, gazing at the scene below.

"Lemmings?" tried Percy.

"No!" snapped Cuthbert. "Balaclava, Balaclava."

"Why?" wailed Percy in despair. "Everyone knows who we are."

Something blue flashed between them causing Cuthbert to look where it came from instead of where it was going. "What was that?"

"How would I know?" said Percy, looking in the same direction as his questioner.

Jasper leapt to his feet and waved his arm above his head. "Now!" he shouted "Pull!"

All along the sides of the track, members of the Valley mafia pulled the fishing line tight, expecting to unseat Nurse Brenda. Jasper watched his teams' co-ordinate the effort and smiled. Something flashed past him and the smile froze.

Nurse Brenda pedalled furiously as the first line caught on the make-shift pole in front of her. The fishing line pulled tight and it yanked two of the mafia out of the undergrowth behind her. She smiled at the sound of young heads banging together, and cut the line with the scissors on her handlebars just in time for the next one.

Jasper watched in horror as blue-clad district nurses came from all directions, hurtling down the hills and taking his 'men' by surprise. No-one saw them coming. Mafia members were grabbed by the scruff of the neck and carried down to the track to be swaddled in bandages and dumped in a pile with the fishing line squads.

The squeak of Nurse Brenda's bike changed direction and returned to the ambush site. The sound had concentrated everyone's attention nicely as the well-oiled machines of her cavalry sprung the trap.

A cloud of dust gradually dispersed to reveal several bicycles forming a central laager around the prone figures of the ambush party. The nurses all faced outwards and one of them produced a metal bed pan.

Shouting into the handle, she turned in all directions as the pan amplified her voice. "You may as well come out and join the others. Get it over with quickly and painlessly, or *else*."

Jasper swallowed and, holding up his hands, made the walk of shame towards his captive mafia companions. All eyes were on him as one of the nurses wheeled a bicycle backwards and then closed the gap behind him as he entered the circle.

Nurse Brenda smiled and said, "Don't worry, son, the twins weren't too happy when we rounded them up either."

Cuthbert and Percy independently decided to look where the blue object had actually *gone* and gaped as a line of bicycles moved away with a selection of confused, concussed and contrite Valley mafia members bandaged together in single file.

Percy lifted his hat to help ventilate the top of his head, "So, is this what happened when the lemmings charged the Spartans then?"

"Er, I don't think so, Percy," came the reply.

Chapter Six

It was a subdued Valley mafia that queued outside the Mandrake Arms later that day. Ears were inspected, hair was thoroughly combed and a greenish liquid was forced between many sets of clenched teeth.

Nurse Brenda patrolled along the line of captives and muttered to her assistant, "All this trouble every time and the monsters are as fit as fleas when we get hold of them." She sighed. "It will be the men next."

Percy paced up and down in front of Avril's desk waving one of her blue Biro's in the air to emphasise a point. Occasionally he would put the pen between his lips and strike a Churchillian pose and adopt a deeper voice.

"This was the day when the face of warfare changed forever" he growled, still pacing. "The age of mechanisation has arrived and rendered all foot soldiers obsolete overnight." He clenched the pen between his teeth, sucked hard and declared, "Today in the battle of the Valley, the flower of its youth was decimated; cut down, never to be replaced within the living memory of those of us who survived." He paused for effect. "We shall never forget them. With the dying of the sun, we will remember … are you getting this down, Avril?"

Cuthbert shook his head in wonderment and rolled his eyes heavenwards.

Percy wiped a tear from the corner of both eyes, leaving a blue smudge to match the one around his lips from biting the pen too hard. He peered at Avril. "This is print worthy, you know."

"*Are you insane?*" shrieked Avril, pointing out the window. "All I can see is a line of delinquent children being given a health check by dedicated professionals."

Cuthbert saw his chance. "Ah yes, but did you know that their leader is a potential mass murderer?"

Avril rounded upon him. "Cuthbert, it was a *measles jab* and everyone had one. If I reported every tale I heard about *you*, they would move Fleet Street here to save time and phone calls."

"Tales put about by the misinformed for the unreformed and the partially formed," insisted Cuthbert indignantly.

Percy was so impressed he began writing this quote onto Avril's wall for later use, but she hustled them out before he finished.

"That girl will never make a reporter," grumbled Cuthbert as they walked away past the line of mafia, just as the last one received his green liquid ration.

Percy tapped Nurse Brenda on the shoulder and she turned with a glare. "Got a piece of paper I could borrow, sweetie?" he asked innocently.

Nurse Brenda could change colour like litmus paper as soon as Percy approached, but this time she merely stared in horror. Her expertise rummaged through the filing cabinets of her mind as she noted the blue lips and the dark smudges under Percy's eyes; combined with the vacant stare in Cuthbert's gaze, her fears were confirmed.

"Evacuate girls!" she screamed. "*Code red, code red.*"

The nurses responded instantly and leapt onto their bicycles, heading out of town.

Percy grinned, Cuthbert stared, and the Valley mafia moved in threateningly.

"You couldn't have done that *before* she gave us all that horse ointment, could you, Percy?" snarled Jasper.

Nurse Brenda and her 'flying squad' screeched to a halt outside the new hospital complex and dashed inside to begin the quarantine procedures for the Valley.

This new complex with its twin blocks possessed state of the art communications and the whole country would be on alert within hours. Everywhere with electricity would be alerted. In fact, the only people who wouldn't know about it were those who lived in the Valley.

"Look at that crow," grumbled Nurse Brenda's assistant. "Sits there as if it owns the place. Anyone would think we had built all this just for him."

Chapter Seven

Ronald ambled along behind his brother Henry and the Captain, trying to tune out the constant armchair-warrior conversations between the two of them. Today's subject was Agincourt and the power of the English longbow.

Henry suddenly waded into some bushes and started tearing at the branches with the Captain close behind him.

Ronald sighed and sat on a fallen tree as they argued about the best wood and whether they could laminate something really powerful from growing vegetation. Ronald leant back and dozed happily while they stripped and spliced to their hearts' content; he only awoke when the job was finished and Henry prodded him with the end of a bow.

"You're the weapons expert, care to test it, Ronald?" asked Henry.

Ronald accepted the bow and a newly cut arrow fletched with lord only knew what feathers from a hedgerow. Sighting towards a bunch of white objects on the distant bridge, he drew the bow right back and released the string. The bow gave a mighty twang and the arrow hummed away and out of sight. Seconds later the white objects on the bridge scattered and then reformed.

"Pretty good, Ronald," muttered the Captain. "Whose sheep are those?"

The three of them sauntered towards the bridge to retrieve the arrow, but Ronald began to drop back as they neared their objective. It became clear the 'sheep' were men in white overalls and masks. Ronald dropped into a gully and crept away quickly - he knew a sub-machine gun when he saw it.

Henry had just finished describing the incident to the packed audience in the Mandrake Arms. If it had been anyone other than Henry, no-one would have believed that armed men had stopped them from leaving the Valley.

Mrs Biggle from the Post Office rose shakily to her feet and announced, "That makes sense to me; communications have been down all day. Look ..." She took out her powder compact, flipped open the lid and shouted an order for stamps, covering Cuthbert in powder in the process. Holding the compact up in the air to prove that no reply was forthcoming, she snapped it shut and sat down again.

"Yes, quite," said Henry.

Avril stood and coughed politely. "As the media representative for the Valley, I am sure that I would have been notified of anything like this. They would probably have asked for me to be interviewed by now."

Her smile froze as Mrs Biggle asked excitedly, "Did you write about the helicopter crash, dear?"

"What helicopter crash?" Avril asked nervously.

"The one just before Cuthbert fell down the well and the Valley mafia all attended church."

Avril's impression of a dyslexic goldfish fascinated the audience and they watched as her mouth opened and closed silently. Hesitation became a blur of activity as she grabbed her bag full of notebooks, pads and voice recorders and headed for the exit.

"Did any of that actually happen?" asked Henry, leaning across the women's table.

"On some level, yes," replied Margery. "She only hears odd snatches of conversation from the queue as she bobs up and down under the counter. I'm guessing at something like 'Helluva crop' from one voice mixed with 'nasty rash' from another. 'Cuthbert, nasty fall, are you well?' from someone and 'That left the boys in the lurch' from someone else. See how it works, dear?"

Henry called everyone to relate their experiences of attempting to leave the Valley and they gradually built a comprehensive picture of a complete cordon. Even the tunnel exit at the concrete lake had been boarded over.

One person tried hard to leave several times apparently and was furiously quoting from the Human Rights Act and ticking off every abuse of his rights, until he ran out of fingers.

The locals gradually moved away until he was isolated in the centre of the room, and Henry managed to ask, "Who *are* you?"

The man glanced around nervously, fingers poised in mid-count. His spectacle lenses were so thick that his eyes disappeared when the light caught the glass, and his expression became unreadable.

"Er, Malcolm Masters with a Masters from Maastricht," he said reluctantly. Clearly he much preferred it if his rants went unnoticed.

Henry gasped, "*The* Malcolm Masters, the human rights lawyer?"

"Yes, the one with a Masters from Maastricht," replied the stranger defiantly.

"Four M's, eh, Malcolm?" asked an amused Ronald before Percy entered into the interrogation.

"Okay, Em-Four, watcha doing in the Valley?"

The crowd watched the poor man squirm as his glasses flashed in all directions, before he admitted, "I'm a twitcher."

"Aren't we all?" snapped Percy. "That's probably why Nurse Brenda quarantined the Valley."

Several locals unconsciously scratched various parts of their anatomies as they nodded in agreement.

"Oh, that won't be for long," blurted Malcolm.

"Why not?" asked Henry.

"Because they are going to round us up and make us stay in the new hospital over the hill," the newcomer explained.

Percy panicked. "What about all my stuff?"

"You haven't got any stuff," observed Cuthbert.

"What about the house full of furniture and all those things I don't recognise?" Percy persisted.

"That's *my* stuff," Cuthbert retorted.

Percy leaned forward and patted his hand. "Don't worry, mate," he said soothingly, "I'll look after it, that's what friends are for."

Henry tried to bring things back to somewhere near sensible by asking Malcolm whether the Valley had any interesting birds.

"Huh," muttered Malcolm. "I've been watched by a crow, attacked by a crow, dive bombed by a crow and laughed at by a crow, so the answer to that is ... why do you think I was trying to leave?"

Chapter Eight

The door crashed back on its hinges and much huffing and puffing announced the arrival of the Law.

Constable Beeching squeezed through the door frame muttering about 'subsidence affecting all the doors in the Valley' and stood adjusting his uniform as he scanned the crowd. "Good, you are assembled as per my instructions," he panted.

"What instructions?" asked Ronald; "We always assemble here."

"The instructions I gave to Percy," insisted the constable.

Percy sat on top of a table swinging his legs to diffuse the fumes from his wellies. "Not me constable," he said. "It must have been some other handsome and talented gardener."

The constable took a deep breath and insisted, "I caught you showing photographs of the Valley horse trough to that antiques dealer Martin Hepplewhite for a valuation."

The crowd gasped and stared at Percy as his brain tried to move faster than his mouth before he replied, "I was showing him a photograph of the horse trough, in case I ever found one like it somewhere else."

The crowd swung its attention back to the upholder of the Law.

"Where would you find another one just like it then?"

Percy shrugged and continued to swing his legs. "Simple. Horse troughs were always made in twos, so there will be another around here somewhere."

"How do you know that?" asked the officer suspiciously.

Percy wriggled and Cuthbert looked for a way to escape, but Constable Beeching blocked the only door.

Percy said, "One of my ancestors was a stone mason. During the lull when a Cathedral was finished and all the local lords had built their tombs, he would carve out horse troughs to keep in practice. At some stage people stopped buying his troughs because the horses wouldn't use them, hence the saying 'You can lead a horse to a trough, but you can't make him drink.'" Percy paused and accepted a pint before continuing. "This was embarrassing for my ancestor, so he devised a plan to make them buy two troughs instead of one."

"How?" asked Malcolm in his naivety.

"Well, he realised if one horse began to drink, the other would get jealous and do the same, so he insisted that two troughs were placed near to each other and he would position one horse with its head over the water. Then he would go behind the horse and tug hard on its tail, causing the horse to drop its head to look between its legs to see what he was doing. Of course, the horse hit the water and the other one joined in at the other trough. This also generated another saying; when anyone asked how he managed to sell troughs in pairs, someone would say 'Thereby hangs a tale'."

Percy rummaged around in his welly and produced the slip of paper Beeching had given him to read out in exchange for not arresting him for nearly stealing a horse trough.

The constable gawped and simply blotted out the whole incident.

"I am here to officially inform you that the Valley is in quarantine," he said. "No-one is allowed to leave."

"Shall I serve your meals at the police station then?" asked Marjorie.

"Why?" asked Beeching.

"The pizza parlour is in the next Valley and no-one is allowed to leave," Henry reminded him.

Cuthbert was really depressed. He had been born in the Valley and everyone he knew was in the Valley. True, outsiders did come in, but somehow the Valley seemed to have ways of vetting them before it let them stay.

He still hadn't forgotten the day when he answered a knock on his door. Two huge men stood there and one of them had growled, "Do you want your shed re-tarred?"

Cuthbert had replied, "No thanks," so they took it.

Chapter Nine

The crow awoke to a new day and lifted his sleep mask to check the weather. The mask was in fact a loose feather and it came off and fluttered to the ground below. The crow stretched his wings and walked around inside his nest to free any snagged wing or tail feathers from the twigs and moss décor. These pre-flight checks became the norm after one of his neighbours took off with a wing stuck, pulled his nest with him, and collapsed half the colony.

The crow launched and savoured the ripple in his feathers, which announced he was airborne, and headed for the new blocks in the next valley.

The line of white-clad figures below him merited a look, so he angled downwards just as the first swarm of shotgun pellets hummed past.

Tilting one wing to simulate damage, he fluttered away from the danger and flew back into the Valley fuming.

What sort of nit-wit would shoot at a majestic specimen like him? Shotguns were reserved for those dozy Herbert's, partridges and pheasants so gormless, if left alone to panic, they would all knock each other out and litter the ground without a shot being fired.

He headed for home to call an emergency meeting.

The Valley mafia watched as Jasper banged a stick against the blackboard. The outline of the Valley was marked with crossing points and goat tracks used by the smuggling teams.

"Compromised!" he shouted. "Every one of our routes compromised. We could have made a fortune out of the adults by bringing in supplies." His tone changed dramatically. "This is war, gentlemen; the mafia must reassert itself. Quarter-master, break out the weapons cache."

The quartermaster, otherwise known as 'Stasher' paled. Since the 'old Valley wars' no one had bothered to make new weapons or maintain the battle-damaged gear in the store. The catapults were warped and broken, there were hardly any marbles left for ammunition, and the pea-shooter dried pea ammunition had taken root.

Jasper wracked his brains for a solution as Ronald barged in and sat with them.

Ronald was surrounded by juvenile delinquents who needed some serious training and even more serious ego massaging to become a force to be reckoned with. Ronald stood and studied the map.

"Gentlemen," he said, "I suggest we join forces."

The crow strutted around importantly as all the other crows leaned out of their nests in an attempt to hear him.

His first rabble-rousing sentences had been snatched away by the wind and Cloud Hopper way down on the ground couldn't hear him anyway. After a frantic session of wing semaphore, the rest of the colony surrounded him and balanced either on the rim of his nest or on nearby branches. Cloud Hopper folded a wing around his ear, but still couldn't make anything out from down there.

"Now is the time to stand together, wing to wing," shouted the crow, knocking three birds out of his nest as he gestured.

The nest rocked dangerously.

"Solidarity is the key," he added; accidentally pecking a bird that had always had contact issues.

The ensuing panic sent three more birds overboard. The nest shuddered threateningly.

"We must not be taken by surprise," squawked the crow as the now out of balance nest tipped him out completely.

Cloud Hopper watched as the crow thudded into the forest loam beside him and was touched by the personal visit. He had long been a campaigner for the rights of disabled crows, but his plan for ramps up to each nest had withered when the youngsters used it as a skateboard park. Nudging his visitor, Cloud Hopper asked, "What was all that about then?"

The crow lay on his back; wings spread, and murmured, "Keeping us safe in our nests."

Cloud Hopper looked up and judged the distance his visitor had fallen. "Wow," he said, "some presentation."

Chapter Ten

Margery wiped the inside of a glass and surveyed the bar area.

All the usual customers were staring morosely into a tumbler and contemplating a bleak future. It only needed the pub to run out of crisps for a riot to break out.

Smiling mischievously, she said, "You know, Cuthbert, I remember Aunt Liza telling me about your mother telling her about a hospital visit she made with you when you were little."

After a communal shudder at the mention of Aunt Liza, everyone focused upon Cuthbert and his legendary ability to hide all emotions behind a neutral façade.

Margery continued, "It wasn't this fancy new place, of course; it was the old gothic pile with turrets and big iron gates. Apparently you were met by a group of nurses wearing latex aprons and gloves and, being young, your speech wasn't fully developed and you ran out screaming 'Argh, look out, wubber women'."

The bar exploded into laughter at someone else's expense and soon the comments began.

"You'll never erase that memory, Cuthbert."

"Couldn't you just have rubbed shoulders with them?"

"Don't worry, you'll soon bounce back."

Margery smiled, the mood was lifted and her landlady skills were intact.

Cuthbert muttered, "All right for you lot, those wubber women were weally weird."

Constable Beeching was sweating. The Valley mafia weren't supposed to be here; it was Ronald who had invited him for 'a chat.' He sat precariously on a chair with his backside hanging over each side like saddlebags.

Ronald interrogated him and the mafia formed a circle around them watching every move.

"Right, Beeching," began Ronald, "you were sent here to tell us about the Valley being put into quarantine. What else did you hear?"

"Nothing," stammered the Constable. "That's all they told me. I expected to be at home now."

Ronald persisted. "You must have seen something useful or heard some of the planning. Think, man."

Beeching sweated some more. "If I had, I would have told you. Don't forget, as a policeman I'm a professional observer."

Ronald and the mafia sneered in unison at this remark. The entire Valley relied upon Beeching's incompetence to survive.

"What's the point of bottling us up in here?" asked Ronald nastily. "What's the next step?"

Beeching insisted he had only heard from Nurse Brenda that 'Once they are in the new hospital, they are at our mercy'."

Ronald paced. "How will they get us all there, though?" he mused. Stopping suddenly, he faced the officer with his hand sliding menacingly into an inside pocket. "What else did you hear? Last chance, Plod," he snarled, doing his best James Cagney impression.

Beeching panicked. "Nothing, really; I couldn't hear anything above the noise of the helicopters."

Ronald pounced. "Helicopters, what helicopters?"

The Constable's words erupted like a burst from a machine gun. "Helicopters, great big ones. Four of them. We couldn't see for dust and the noise was terrible."

Ronald turned to his audience. "That's it, they are going to bring in helicopters and take us all out of the Valley together."

Jasper looked at his feet. "That's it then. We can't fight helicopters.

Ronald snorted, "'Course we can, lads. I've been here before and it's simple. We just tie a cow to each one when it lands."

The mafia gaped in wonderment at their new hero.

The men had wandered off in groups, a sure sign trouble was brewing.

Margery came out from behind the bar and joined the ladies. "Are they starting another resistance movement, Elspeth?"

The Captain, Elspeth's husband, had left with the rest, so she replied, "Oh, I expect so, Margery. It will be all maps and booby traps for a day or two before they get hungry and come home."

Margery sighed. "Strange things men - generous and grown-up one minute and dozy as meat flies the next."

Elspeth looked startled. She had never heard the words 'generous' and 'men' used in the same sentence before.

"Is Henry generous then?" she asked.

Margery had a distant look in her eyes as she answered. "I wasn't thinking of Henry, dear. An ex-lover of mine once gave me a mink, though."

Elspeth stared. "Lucky you."

Margery shuddered. "Oh, I hated it."

Elspeth stared harder. "I'll have it then."

Margery patted her hand gently. "You would have hated it too, dear; nasty, snappy little thing, it was."

"The lover or the mink?" asked Geraldine.

"Both," Margery smirked.

"Women can be strange too, you know," said Percy from behind the bar where his empty glass had miraculously filled itself. "I remember when my mate's wife was suspecting."

The women squeezed their eyes shut and collectively hoped they could make him disappear using concentrated feminine wiles.

Margery ignored the elephant in the room and tried for the armadillo. "Don't you mean 'expecting', Percy?"

"Oh, no," said Percy, settling onto a bar stool and shuffling. "She was always suspecting something. "If he was out late, or he'd spent money on new clothes, or one of her dresses was missing, it was always something."

The women exchanged desperate glances. No-one could see where this headed, so they sat staring at him, which all the encouragement Percy needed for another shuffle.

"My mate was an undercover policeman, needed different disguises and kept strange hours, but he couldn't tell her anything because of the official secrets act. Anyway, one night they had a tip-off about a load of smuggled Aspirin. This gang had been giving them a real headache and the cops needed some for themselves. They staked out the docks and waited for the gang to arrive and open the container. My mate borrowed a dress from his wife's wardrobe, and a wig and high heels from a mannequin at the lost and found office as a disguise. Just as the moon appeared and illuminated the scene, the gang came and started unloading the container onto a lorry. The police cordon began to close in and the helicopters arrived overhead."

"What happened?" gasped Avril, leaning forward.

Percy leant forward as well to ratchet up the tension, and continued, "Well, the downdraft from the helicopters blew my mate's wig off and sent him chasing after it along the pier. The other coppers thought it was a lookout escaping and gave chase, so the helicopters followed them and everyone ended up at the railings right at the end. That's when my mate broke down sobbing and had a nervous breakdown as the gang escaped. It just shows you must never underestimate pier pressure."

The women weren't sure how long Percy had been gone, because he seemed to disappear during a lull in reality and took time with him.

They jumped as the door slammed back against the wall and Arkle entered, dragging a flattened and badly crumpled space-suit behind her.

"Don't panic ladies," she boomed. "Aliens have surrounded the Valley, but don't worry; if it bleeds, we can kill it."

She threw the suit across a table like a discarded snake skin and studied it as if planning to turn it into a scarf.

Margery glanced from the suit to Arkle and back again. "Er, was there anything inside it, dear?"

Chapter Eleven

The space-suited men in the cordon had huddled together for protection. They had been warned about the Valley mafia and the strange inhabitants, but no-one mentioned artillery. They had all been facing inwards to where the threat was.

Suddenly several of the white clad figures went down exactly like nine-pins and one poor chap disappeared altogether. It was no good shouting at each other to pass the blame, because it only made their visors steam up, so they sent up a flare for reinforcements.

Jasper had been watching this from the hillside inside his bush. He saw Arkle and her giant horse skittle the cordon and one scrawny chap ran away in his boxer shorts after she had grabbed his suit as a trophy.

The cordon was quickly reinforced and it stayed in place.

Jasper rubbed his chin where stubble should be in a few years and headed back to the village.

Arkle swung her head from Margery to Avril and back again. "Quarantine, what quarantine?"

Avril explained that Percy had been in her office sucking a ball-point pen and smeared blue ink under his eyes and then left looking like the living dead.

"It can be arranged," interrupted Arkle gleefully.

The ensuing silence was caused by the women imagining a one-sided battle between Arkle and Percy, but Margery was forced to bring them back to reality. "The thing is, ladies, this quarantine is still being arranged and we don't know how long they intend to keep us at this new hospital."

Elspeth entered the discussion as she considered that the problem simply wasn't that big. "Does it really matter? We spend most of our time together anyway and at least the meals would be provided."

Several of the women nodded in agreement, until Margery shrieked, "Think about it, ladies, it's not just us forming a knitting circle, it involves *Cuthbert and Percy*!"

Arkle was appalled by her own lack of femininity and muttered, "They're not the only ones who can't knit."

Margery turned to Arkle with the glint of battle in her eyes. "How many horses can you round up dear? *Tomorrow we ride!*"

Jasper was addressing his 'men'. They knew the Valley and its tunnel system like the backs of their hands, but if they risked washing them, there was a chance the felt-tip plan would come off as well.

"As usual, we can't rely upon the adults to solve this one. By the time the men have drawn up plans and the women have chosen their outfits, it will be too late."

The men gathered around Cuthbert's table and as usual compared each other's impressions of the tunnel system, and scrapped the result when nothing matched up.

There was a blast of heat as all the crumpled pieces of paper spontaneously combusted close to the cooking range.

Ronald sat back with a nonchalant air. He had fought in secret wars all over the world in clandestine locations. Most of them were secret because he didn't know how to pronounce them. "All we do is create a diversion at one point, and then the rest of us can escape when they're pre-occupied."

"The rest of us?" queried the Captain. "You're not part of the diversion then?"

Ronald smiled wolfishly. "Oh no, I'll be needed for the later stages of the operation. You always find someone expendable for the diversion."

Somehow his eyes managed to rest on Cuthbert and Percy at exactly the same time.

Henry had been puzzling over something for a while. "How do they know where all the tunnel exits are? Not even the Valley mafia knows all of them." He made a mental note to ask Marjorie, as his wife seemed to see through mysteries quicker than he did.

Cuthbert quickly looked at Percy and asked, "Expendable - does that mean they're going to stretch our abilities?"

Percy replied, "Nah, that's extendable, that is. Hang on, who said expendable?"

Ronald sniggered and drew the glare of all Percy's ancestors onto himself.

"I'll have you know that my family have been the backbone of our military throughout history," Percy began.

Ronald counter-attacked. "Huh, forget to pass it on, did they? Is that why your hat is so close to your belt buckle?"

Henry stepped in before the squabbling reached the stage where Percy reached into his welly for a turnip, and asked, "Does anyone have a plan?"

The silence, as all the great minds did everything but think, was interrupted by a gentle scraping sound as Percy moved the butter dish and pepper pots into formation on the table top. He then sat back and admired his handiwork.

"Is that the plan?" asked the Captain looking at the butter dish flanked by the pepper pots.

"If you like," replied Percy, "but if you squint and look from a certain angle, it looks just like the Taj Mahal."

Chapter Twelve

The next morning found a group of horses tied to the bronze bell outside The Mandrake Arms. They stamped and shook their heads aggressively, causing the air from their flaring nostrils to form clouds of steam, until Arkle appeared and then they all stood demurely and transformed into themselves into show ponies.

Now that the animals were under control, Arkle strode into the bar to create the same effect amongst the humans.

The first person she saw was Percy balancing a turnip on his nose. Apparently he demonstrated the fact that if Isaac Newton hadn't used an apple his theory wouldn't have worked.

Ronald sidled up to Percy with his hand in his pocket as if was about to substitute the turnip for a hand grenade, and Cuthbert was convinced his three-legged bar stool signalled an earthquake warning.

As usual the women tended to congregate on one side and the men on the other, so Marjorie stepped into 'No-man's-land' and waited for her husband Henry to finish one of his anecdotes directed at Constable Beeching.

"So you see Constable," Henry was saying, "escaped prisoners are creatures of habit. If you want to find them, check the bars."

A ripple of laughter followed, but Constable Beeching was having none of it. "If he had been under the care of a professional like me, the bars would have been checked and he wouldn't have got out in the first place."

Henry stared at the policeman, but could find no hint of humour in the face before him.

Luckily Marjory stepped in with "I see the horses are outside, dear. Are we sticking to last night's plan?"

She suddenly had the attention of all the men. A plan, agreed without the participation of the accumulated wealth of experience the men could offer? It was unheard of.

Arkle stepped into the centre of the room. "Well," she barked, "nothing is set in stone, but ..."

Cuthbert stopped rocking on the three-legged stool and coughed politely.

Everyone in the room froze.

Cuthbert never contradicted anyone ever and especially not Arkle. Now that he was the centre of attention, there was nowhere for Cuthbert's mind to retreat to, so he pushed ahead. "My graveyard is full of slabs with words written in stone."

Arkle watched him as if his devious thoughts would be displayed on his forehead, but then she remembered who this was and asked menacingly, "Is there room for one more?"

Cuthbert lowered his head as rebellion wasn't his forte. "Sorry, Ar …"

The temperature in the room dropped and glasses of liquid were scooped up as if the Marshall had just entered the saloon in Dodge City.

"Ar …?" rumbled Arkle.

Everyone had expected this moment to come, but somehow they all pictured it being Percy.

Cuthbert looked around wildly.

"It's Pirates' Day today," shouted Percy, coming to his friend's rescue.

"Pirates' Day?" asked Arkle incredulously.

"Arr," said Percy.

"Arr," said Henry.

"Arr," said the Captain.

"Apparently," said Marjory with a sigh.

Henry finally caught Marjorie behind the bar and asked her about the tunnel exits being covered so effectively.

Marjorie glanced from Henry to Cuthbert and back again. She paused whilst Ronald and Mrs Biggle sidled up to join them and then explained. "This feud goes back a long way. Have you ever heard about Aunt Liza …"

A shudder went through the group.

"… cutting the feet off Cuthbert's jelly babies, so they would stand up for her to shoot at them with an air-rifle?"

Everyone nodded. Cuthbert's deprived childhood was full of tales like this.

Marjorie continued. "Well, Brenda was a friend of Aunt Liza."

Another shudder.

"They played at the farm together. Brenda always wanted to be a nurse and developed a scheme where she and Liza would suck the colour out of Cuthbert's Jelly-babies so they looked ill, and then make beds out of match-boxes to play at hospitals. Cuthbert has never forgiven either of them and every time Nurse Brenda offers him any treatment, he thinks she is going to suck the colour out of him."

The men turned and gaped at Cuthbert and he waved cheerily in return.

"But the tunnels?" prompted Henry.

Mrs Biggle took up the story. "Nurse Brenda is a Valley girl - she's old Valley-folk and she was in the Valley mafia long ago. She knows all the tunnels, dear."

A pot plant in the corner snorted and Margery patted the uppermost leaf saying, "This may hurt, Jasper, but the girls *started* the Valley mafia."

The pot-plant visibly wilted.

Cuthbert watched as the women gathered to discuss breaching the cordon around the Valley. It would be a mounted cavalry charge and Elspeth likened it to the charge of the light brigade, until she remembered that Arkle was leading it. None of the ladies wanted to go down in history as being part of the heavy brigade, so she just sighed and paid attention.

Cuthbert now focused on the table surrounded by men and it was his turn to sigh; he had always felt left out of things. As the undertaker's son the other kids only wanted him when there were trenches to be dug for war games. Now he watched as the men leaned in towards each other. Remarkably, Percy was the centre of attention. Cuthbert gaped as the men hung on to Percy's every word and patted him on the back when he stood to fetch 'something calming' for everyone before the attack.

"You seem popular and involved in things," noted Cuthbert through gritted teeth. "What's going on?"

Percy tapped the side of his nose. "Need to know basis, Cuthbert, need to know," and he smirked.

Cuthbert rocked back slightly on his three-legged stool until the short leg rested on the toe of Percy's welly and then shifted his weight.

Percy's face began to change colour and he gasped, "Not the seed collection, don't damage the seed collection."

Cuthbert eased the pressure slightly and asked politely, "Well, do I need to know?"

Percy glared at him and lifted one foot to rub his toe. He glanced around for security reasons and said, "This is for your ears only, mate."

"And mine," said Belinda from behind the bar.

"And mine," said Jasper from behind the pot plant.

Percy's shoulders slumped as he gave up, but then he remembered his own importance and started arranging glasses and packets of peanuts on the bar to represent the plan. "I have the most important role of the operation," he began. "I'm the shock trooper who will start the action off."

"Somebody will definitely get a shock," muttered Jasper.

Percy ignored him and continued, "It's my job to run straight at the cordon, setting off the trip-wires and flares to make the German Shepherds chase me."

He sat back smugly waiting for the applause.

Cuthbert exchanged a glance with the pot plant, but he wasn't sure Jasper was still there. "Aren't you worried?"

Percy snorted his contempt. "What chance is there of a bunch of foreign sheep herders in leather shorts catching me?"

Cuthbert felt much better now.

Chapter Thirteen

The ladies lined up outside and stroked the horses, as the horses sized them up for capabilities and a bit of a giggle later on.

The one chosen by Arkle was ready for the off, preferably without her on its back.

Margery swung effortlessly into the saddle and her horse reared and gently pawed the air to everyone's delight, except Arkle's.

"How does she always come across as Lady Guinevere?" she muttered.

The men had commandeered Percy's tractor and were hanging onto the sides with various weapons salvaged by the Captain from the Northwest Frontier. They promised to not start the engine until the horses had a head start, and Ronald worried the vibrations might set off the array of devices hidden in his tactical suit.

Percy limbered up ready for his dash. He had stretched his calf muscles, which involved waking them from a long sleep, and hidden his seed collection in his pockets, so they wouldn't slip between his toes; he loved the attention as he tested wind direction and wrote his blood group on a label on his lapel, until a kick up the backside from Ronald sent him off in roughly the right direction.

Arkle signalled for the horses to advance and Marjorie, Elspeth, Avril and Geraldine formed into line and moved ahead behind Percy.

Percy began to realise that being a pretend gardener was no substitute for being fit and started to slow until he felt the earth tremble, and glanced back. Arkle had signalled the horses into a trot and they were catching up rapidly. He began to wish his wellies had spurs.

The horses were now in a loose 'V' formation with Arkle leading; she had just signalled 'Increase to gallop' and she threw in 'Lower lances' for good measure. The earth shook.

Percy risked another glance back just as he triggered the first flare and he disappeared in a cloud of smoke. Disorientated, he changed course slightly, which was a good thing, because he left the smoke behind, but now he could see the dogs.

"Dogs, nobody mentioned dogs. Where are the German Shepherds in leather shorts?" he ranted to himself as his breath began to realise just how out of tune his lungs were.

The foxhunter Arkle rode was really in its element; it had been a long time since it was in a real chase. At that moment the smoke appeared and a scruffy apparition appeared from it, just as the sun caught a flash of red hair.

"Fox!" screamed the elemental instinct in both Arkle and the horse and they changed course in pursuit.

Percy now detonated thunder-flashes and smoke at regular intervals until the scene looked like an early newsreel filmed on the Somme. He risked another glance behind; Arkle was coming to his rescue, but why had the dogs formed into a pack and why was she shouting "Tally-Ho"?

The adrenaline rush traditionally felt by his ancestors at times like these overcame him, but then it occurred to him that there may be a reason why they were all ancestors and not living relatives. His little legs pumped faster.

The Captain had been trusted with the tractor controls and his crew felt decidedly under the weather. Between dropping into dips and lurching sideways as the tracks bit into thin air, it was like being on a North Atlantic convoy; in fact, sighting Murmansk would have been the highlight of the trip.

Percy's heart pumped fit to burst, when he recognised a clanking sound. "My tractor," he gasped, "coming to the rescue, I'm saved," and fell flat on his face, which was fortunate because the Captain hadn't seen him in the smoke and the tracks went both sides of him. One of his wellies caught on the trailer hitch dragging him along behind.

Percy's scent was immediately lost amongst the diesel fumes and Arkle and her pack split away each side and passed the tractor in another cloud of smoke.

The Captain shouted over the din, "No sign of Percy, chaps. He must have got through; he can fetch help now."

Back at the Mandrake Arms, the gathering was buoyant. Everyone seemed to have forgotten that Percy was only the diversion and they should have breached the cordon instead.

The dogs lay outside gasping or slurping noisily at the water bowls Marjorie had laid out and even the tractor seemed to be creaking with exertion.

Arkle glanced at the horses gathered around the water trough and frowned. "Why aren't they drinking?"

Cuthbert piped up with, "You can take a horse to water, but you can't make it drink, Ar ..."

"Ar?" snarled Arkle.

"He meant '*Are* you going to do anything about it', dear," said Marjorie with a warning glance at Cuthbert.

Cuthbert nodded mutely like a gargoyle about to fall off a church tower.

"Can't make them drink, eh? We'll see," muttered a determined Arkle.

Glancing across, Henry asked, "Are those Percy's wellies sticking out of the trough?"

Everyone moved from different angles to surround the trough and, sure enough, the wellies were sticking out and Percy lay face down in the bottom. He had drunk it dry, right down to the algae.

"Oh, good grief, Percy," boomed Arkle, "we gave you one simple task; even Lassie could fetch help when they needed her to."

Percy lifted one arm that resignedly collapsed again as everyone walked away.

Nurse Brenda listened carefully to the reports of the attempted breakout and decided to accelerate the schedule. She lifted a special telephone and uttered a code word.

The Valley mafia had been on the hill top watching this calamitous attempt and they shook their heads in unison.

"Well," said Jasper, "we won't be awarding the MBE to any of the adults anytime in the near future."

"MBE?" queried Malcolm Masters with a Masters from Maastricht, who hadn't been allowed anywhere near the action.

"Medal Belonging to Edgar," chanted the mafia.

The men gathered around a table near the bar and silently assessed the day's work; it was a silent assessment, because no one had anything to brag about.

Ronald slammed down his empty glass and announced, "Right, it's time to get back to basics. What we need is twenty-four hours surveillance. We are surrounded by a cordon of men in bio-hazard suits and they must do a shift change and be replaced by a new team at set periods, so we will establish an observation point and work in relays until we have logged all movements and established a pattern. Gentlemen, to the upstairs windows."

Cuthbert and Percy trailed behind because they were usually excluded from anything involving 'gentlemen'. Feeling rather silly, the men followed Ronald upstairs and watched as he arranged a table and chair in front of the attic window. Apparently this was where he stored most of his equipment and, after rummaging about in various camouflage-patterned bergens and rucksacks, he settled down at the table with a pair of binoculars on a tripod.

"Right," Ronald announced, "we log all movements and time any shift change; then we can take advantage of gaps in procedure."

Ronald obviously had his mercenary hat on, so everyone watched carefully ready to learn.

Percy found a bandolier of what looked like pens amongst Ronald's gear, and slung it over his shoulder.

"Paper," said Ronald, snapping his fingers.

Percy reached into his welly and pulled out a folded sheet, which promptly sagged like a dying flower recorded by time-lapse photography as soon as it experienced fresh air.

Henry laid a pristine sheet of headed notepaper in front of his brother and smirked at Percy.

"Pen," snapped Ronald, but before Henry could ease his gold retirement present from its mafia-proof clip, Percy delved into Ronald's equipment bandolier and placed something into the outstretched hand.

Ronald grunted his thanks and pressed the end to release the ball-point causing the whole room to fill with smoke. "Not that one, you idiot," he spluttered, so Percy handed him another one, which managed to shoot CS gas right into Ronald's face.

"Argh!" said Ronald, so Percy handed him yet another one.

The men could see this going on for some time, and quietly made their escape back down to the bar.

Ronald was left with Percy as his assistant and because his eyes were streaming from the gas, it was Percy on duty with the binoculars.

"See anything?" Ronald asked through gritted teeth and running eyes.

Percy shrugged. "Just a bunch of blokes in bio-degradable suits standing in a line."

"Bio-hazard suits, nitwit," snapped Ronald. "It's to stop them catching what you've got."

"Charisma?" suggested Percy.

Jasper paced in front of his troops; this cordon was becoming a nuisance. What was the point of stealing stuff in one valley, if you couldn't reach the other valley to sell it?

Ronald found that his eyes gradually cleared, but there seemed to be blurred figures moving at the back of the room. He didn't believe in ghosts, or at least he hoped they didn't exist, because a fair number of them would be looking for *him*.

He was impressed by Percy though; he had never taken his eyes off the Valley and the sheet of paper was covered in writing.

"Percy," he whispered, "is there someone else in the room?"

A gentle snoring sound shattered all of Ronald's illusions and suddenly the blurred figures were taping him to the chair and he felt a bag slide over his head. It was no good trying to talk, because the bag sucked in and out like a bellows and he needed the air. Shaking his head slightly, he managed to find a rip in the bag where he saw blurred figures lift a blurred Percy onto another chair and pat him on the head. *He didn't even wake up!*

Jasper surveyed the scene, shook his head and sat in the chair with a pen and some fresh paper.

Now let's do this job properly, he thought after studying Percy's doodles of flowers and funny-shaped vegetables.

Chapter Fourteen

The following morning found the Valley mafia in the bar nursing lemonade, with Ronald and the rest of the men glaring at them.

Percy had greeted everyone cheerily and announced that "this surveillance lark could leave you really refreshed" until he recognised the expression on Ronald's face and the whiteness of his knuckles.

Jasper waved several sheets of paper in the air. "Gentlemen, this is a comprehensive itinerary of the movements of the cordon last night. We took it in shifts and had 'eyes-on' the target at all times. We never actually saw any of the funny-shaped vegetables spotted by Percy, but we did spot an anomaly."

The adults reluctantly took the sheaf of papers from Jasper and the Captain studied them. He turned them over and studied them some more. "They're all blank," he spluttered.

Ronald guffawed, "Hah, so much for the great Valley mafia, how do you explain blank reports then, oh great surveillance experts?"

Jasper waited patiently until the sniggers died down before saying, "The sheets are blank because nothing happened. Nobody moved and there was no shift change. The only event was that one of the men fell over when blind-Pugh mistook him for a sheep and he is still lying there three and a half hours later."

The absolute certainty on Jasper's face quelled any argument and the men looked at each other in turn for inspiration.

The women had gradually filed in quietly and heard about the night's work, but could offer no explanation. Explaining the actions of one man was difficult enough, but when it came to a whole field full, well, even Marjorie had her limits.

Jasper looked around the assembly and sighed. "Fortunately we have found something that may help to solve this riddle."

"Oh-oh," said Percy, jumping up. "Is it the one where a man escapes from a padded cell with only a hairgrip and a plastic spoon?"

"Wasn't it a needle and a ball of wool?" asked Cuthbert.

"When I was in the East," began the Captain.

Everyone's attention returned to Jasper as he slammed a crossbow down onto the table.

"'Ere, that's mine," said Ronald indignantly.

"It was," smiled Jasper. "Now it's part of your contribution to the mafia benevolent fund." His words were punctuated by the thuds and clicks of more of Ronald's weaponry being placed on table tops in front of mafia members.

Ronald fumed and Percy jabbered on about how the riddle hadn't been explained yet.

Chapter Fifteen

Outside, it was a beautiful clear morning and everyone assembled at the edge of the field. The sight of the modern crossbow inspired Geraldine and she had dashed to the museum to bring another example and some extra bolts.

Jasper stretched and limbered up ready for action and the men took it in turns to try to wind the handles on Geraldine's medieval offering.

"Oh, for heaven's sake," snorted Arkle, snatching the weapon away from Ronald and winding both handles effortlessly. "That's how it's done, man."

Raising the ancient weapon to her shoulder, she fired. The bolt left the Valley in a blur and if it made a landfall, no one saw it. In fact, if it had happened many years ago, it would have explained the sinking of the Titanic or the Hindenburg disaster.

Jasper took aim at one of the figures in the white suits, just as the women closed in to stop him from having to run the mafia from inside prison, but the bolt was on its way!

All eyes focused on one of the figures as it wobbled and then shot skywards. Jasper reloaded and repeated the performance with the same effect on the next one.

A mixed chorus of "What, how, why and cool, can I have a go?" greeted his efforts, and Jasper handed the bow to Ronald.

"Just as I thought," he said with a smile, "they're inflatable. I saw them all rock in sequence when the wind sprang up - probably Government cut-backs."

The rest of the day was spent running around retrieving bolts and taking it in turns to widen the gap in the balloon cordon.

Somehow, Percy was having to run faster than anyone; how Ronald could keep mistaking him for a chap in a white suit was beyond him.

Nurse Brenda was furious, she had the biggest and strangest outbreak of her career on her hands and some bean-counter had axed the cordon and replaced it with balloon animals. Checking the syringes tucked into the bun at the back of her head, she stormed into the corridor and began to pick up speed.

Now, Oliver Ogden the hospital manager was a man in a position of power. He had a desk and a chair and a window and the ability to thwart all those who actually achieved something in life.

Having enrolled in medicine because he wanted to wear a white coat, and because no one had let him, he followed the 'suit-route' until he could wreak his revenge upon those who opened people up and then claimed the credit for curing them. Ridiculous! None of that stuff could happen without the likes of him and if they left him to it, the paperwork would take that long to complete, the illness would have passed anyway, one way or another.

He knew he was popular did Oliver Ogden, because as he passed the lesser mortals in the corridors, he would hear them mutter "Oh-oh." You don't get a nickname or called by your initials without being popular; now do you?

Oliver managed to jump and look startled whilst at the same time study the contents of his coffee cup somersaulting over his desk as Nurse Brenda crashed into his office.

The SAS had once visited the Valley and copied the mafia's 'Horns of the buffalo' manoeuvre and the district nurses' door-breaching techniques. Having stolen both, they retreated to Hereford and put razor wire around the camp because the Valley folk knew where they lived.

Oliver was tempted to jump to his feet, but this would only leave him level with Brenda's belt buckle, so he retained his position of authority and quaked. His authoritative "Can I help you?" came out as a squeak.

Brenda sneered, "Only when I need paperclips buster. Who removed the cordon?"

Another squeak. "Cordon?"

Brenda leaned forward over his desk. "The cordon around the Valley, you unctuous little worm, who removed it?"

Oliver retrieved a now sodden piece of paper from the swamp on his desk top and it flopped around his hand as he tried to wave it "Do you know how much it was costing?" he squeaked.

Brenda slowly removed a syringe from her hair and asked silkily, "Do you know how much one of these costs? It is very little and yet it eradicates ninety-nine percent of all known twerps."

Oliver fainted clean away.

Brenda squirted the glucose solution into her mouth; dealing with clowns like this was thirsty work. Leaving the syringe stuck upright and wobbling menacingly for when he woke up, Brenda left the room.

Chapter Sixteen

In the bar of the Mandrake Arms, the atmosphere had settled down from celebratory to merely highly satisfied. Every now and again someone would snigger at the thought of punctured white suits hurtling upwards.

"Well, that was fun," said Henry, stretching his arms. "What now?"

"Simple," barked the Captain. "We've won; now we can leave the Valley."

"But we don't go anywhere," Brenda pointed out. "We never leave the Valley."

The atmosphere deflated as surely as the men in white suits had, and everyone gradually wandered off to their respective homes.

Walking back to Cuthbert's farm, Percy suddenly asked, "Is that it then - have we beaten Nurse Brenda?"

Cuthbert paused and shuddered. "No-one beats Nurse Brenda," he said in a hollow tone. "Do you remember old farmer Farmer?"

Percy stopped walking. "Farmer, Farmer? Did he plant baby chaps in flat caps and then harvest them when they were ripe?"

"No, his name was Farmer and he was a farmer," said Cuthbert. "Just like a man named Weaver made baskets."

"So the Farmer was a basket case? No wonder he needed Nurse Brenda," argued Percy.

Cuthbert sighed as the drama drained out of his tale. "Old Farmer sent for Nurse Brenda because he had a pain in his leg and I heard her threaten him. Less than two days later, I buried him."

Percy was shocked; murder had come to ruin this idyllic Valley and that was his job.

They carried on walking and Percy asked, "What did she say?"

"I heard her say that she would be back tomorrow and she would be bringing someone with her to solve it once and for all and that it would be the last time he would bother her. The next day old farmer Farmer fell into his baling machine and I had to bury him wrapped in baling twine and with one leg missing."

Percy looked around wildly as if expecting dramatic music to end the story. "Back to the Mandrake Arms," he cried. "Alert the others."

Ronald and his brother Henry were still in the bar because they lived there and this was the home they would have wandered off to if they had wandered off.

Marjorie was there for the same reason and Belinda was there because she worked behind the bar.

Cuthbert and Percy collided in the doorway gasping for breath and Marjorie automatically slid two glasses across the counter.

"Nurse Brenda murdered farmer Farmer and put him in a basket," gasped Percy.

"Quick, save yourselves. We'll hold her off," gasped Cuthbert, causing his friend to look at him and then look for another basket.

Marjorie intervened calmly and diplomatically. "What are you loons blathering about?"

Cuthbert spluttered out his story as Percy sipped at something he suspected had just been used to clean the pumps out. Cuthbert ended his tale and looked expectantly from one to the other.

Margery shook her head. "Cuthbert, whenever anyone mentions Nurse Brenda, you lose all sense of reason. The reason Farmer had a pain in his leg was because it was a wooden one and it was chafing. Nurse Brenda was bringing someone with a state of the art false leg, so the problem would never happen again. She told him to wait until it came, but the old fool tapped his pipe out on the wooden one, set fire to it and fell into the baling machine trying to stamp the flames out."

Ronald had to leave the room and could be heard roaring with laughter.

Henry's reporter's instincts told him this wasn't over yet, so he stayed, and anyway, he was fascinated by the green foam coming from Percy's mouth. It looked like the chemical they used to clean the pumps with.

Cuthbert stared at the door and slowly backed into a corner.

It was Nurse Brenda and she focused upon Cuthbert like a mongoose with a cobra. "This isn't over yet, Cuthbert," she hissed (proving Henry's instincts). "You haven't heard the last of me."

Then, spinning around to face Percy, she recoiled at the sight of the green foam and bubbles. "Code red, er, green; it's phase two," she screamed into her phone and ran for her bike.

"Oh dear, here we go again," said Marjory as Percy held his glass up for a refill and Brenda's bike squeaked maniacally into the distance.

Chapter Seventeen

Sirens sounded throughout the hospital, the droning sound chasing down the corridors and turning it into a demented beehive. Heads popped out of doorways and then disappeared before medical ethics grabbed them by the conscience and made them take part in an emergency.

Bemused patients were told they were cured and going home that afternoon, but could they return the drips and oxygen bottles as soon as possible please.

Oliver Ogden's phone had taken on a life of its own, staff queries, press queries and even patients association queries.

Patients, did they have associations? He didn't even know they communicated, he thought they just lay there groaning.

Those surgeon chaps had been at his door in their masks, gowns and silly rubber boots asking for casualty predictions and whether the helicopter pad was clear.

Helicopter pad, did they have one? If he'd known that he would have left his car at home and laughed at the traffic jams below. What on earth had that Nurse Brenda triggered now?

Nurse Brenda was briefing her troops; they stood in two lines as she paced in front of them outlining the situation.

"Unfortunately this epidemic has broken out amongst some of the most awkward civilians on the planet. You will all have experienced the Valley folk at some time, I assume?"

The gasps and sideways glances confirmed this was so and a frisson of apprehension ran through the ranks.

A hand appeared above the heads of the front rank and Nurse Brenda paused. "Step to the front, but don't expect to be excused, we're all in this together ... oh, it's you, Penelope Newgirl."

"Newton," the girl corrected sunnily. "Penelope Newton."

"Newgirl will do," growled Nurse Brenda. She'd had trouble with this one already "What is it?"

Penelope brightened and asked, "What exactly is this outbreak, because I checked with the office of communicable diseases and there is no record of blue-tinged features suddenly turning green in a red-haired male at any time since records began."

Nurse Brenda was taken aback. A district nurse asking advice from an outside source? It was unheard of. Nurse Brenda began slowly and deliberately so that everyone would know she was in charge.

"We have never needed any office of community diseases to do our job before, have we, ladies? And just because some newly trained girl who thinks a tablet is something you plug in and access Facebook with wants to make a name for herself, it will not change a thing. We rely on the patient's description and our own judgement."

Penelope seized her moment. "Is this patient the red-haired chap who wears turned-down wellies and came to A&E because one of his ancestors was named Arthur and he married Eliza, so he wondered if the building was named after them?"

Chapter Eighteen

Cuthbert and Percy sat at the kitchen table; Percy examined his seed collection, whilst Cuthbert muttered on about Nurse Brenda.

Percy heard it all re-hashed, the tales about Brenda and Aunt Liza (shudder) stealing his jelly babies and cutting the feet off and sucking the colour out so they would look ill and then they could play at hospitals with them, but suddenly even Percy paid attention.

"Would you mind repeating that?" he asked.

Cuthbert knew Percy hadn't been paying attention, so he glared and repeated, "They even pulled the head off my action man and put it on a Barbie so they could have a bearded lady in the circus they made."

"Action Man had a beard?" asked Percy suspiciously.

"Oh yes," said Cuthbert. "It was the explorer; he had a dog-sleigh and a tent."

Percy smirked. "But after that, it was just a bearded lady loitering within tent?"

Margery had sent Belinda home and was finishing off the bar work when the Captain came in to join Henry and Ronald at their table. "Is it all over then?" he asked.

Ronald shrugged, but Henry sighed and replied, "I don't think so. From what Margery tells me, Nurse Brenda doesn't give up that easily."

Margery laughed. "She doesn't give up at all; the Valley mafia have had more trouble with her than they have with all the police forces put together. She once tried to pump nit-powder down the tunnels because she was too short-staffed to round them all up."

Henry smiled. "For a Valley lost in time and geography, we really do have our adventures, don't we?"

An equable silence descended on the bar, but it didn't reach as far as Cuthbert's kitchen.

Cuthbert was pacing and ranting about the slights and schemes he attributed to Nurse Brenda whilst the cooking range timed him, before it shot out a length of flame.

Percy tried to separate his seed collection. The humidity in his welly was perfect, but it played heck with his filing system. "Did I ever tell you about my ancestor?" he asked.

Cuthbert stopped pacing, causing the oven door to open too early and waste a precision shot of blue flame. "Would that be the one who lost the battle of Troy because he put the wooden horse on double yellow lines and it was towed away, or the one who tried to tether the Hindenburg Airship to an electricity pylon instead of its mooring mast?" Cuthbert was in no mood for Percy at the moment and he stormed out, oblivious to another blue flame missing him by mere atoms as he went by.

Inside one of his outbuildings, Cuthbert banged and crashed about under the guise of rearranging things. He was seething about Nurse Brenda. She seemed to have haunted him all his life and was regularly featured in his nightmares along with Aunt Liza (shudder).

Percy was unaffected by his friend's departure, but he couldn't help wondering if the Valley was about to change. This tension wasn't good for the dynamics of the complicated relationships involved where, of course, Percy was at the head of the game and the others all aspired to be him. He sighed and scooped up his seed collection before carefully shaking it into his welly and squeezing his foot in to keep everything firmly in place. Then he went in search of Cuthbert.

He found him in one of the outbuildings. Cuthbert didn't excel at expressions, but he did 'morose' rather well.

Percy spotted a coffin on trestles and tried several times to launch himself so that he could sit on top of it. After failing several times, he struck a pose meant to imply that the performance had been deliberate to cheer Cuthbert up. It failed. Percy sighed; this was going to be hard work.

After dragging a box across the room, climbing up and settling down, he discovered Cuthbert had left the building.

Jumping down and causing a spurt of miasma from his shock-absorbing wellies, Percy caught up with Cuthbert in the kitchen. He poured the tea and sat opposite his friend. "You know, mate," began Percy, "things are never as bad as they seem; it's always darkest before the dawn."

"How do you know?" asked Cuthbert.

"Know what?" asked Percy in return.

Cuthbert pressed home his point. "That it's always darkest before the dawn - do you carry a light-meter or something?"

Percy glared at his friend. Sometimes Cuthbert could rival the Sphinx in the enigmatic department and his face was now a blank canvas tempting Percy to turn it into a Jackson Pollock with a blunt instrument. The exchange began as Percy tried the psychological approach.

"It's not me you're angry at, now is it?"

"Yes."

"No, it isn't, you are substituting your anger and redirecting it at me, aren't you?"

"No."

"You won't resolve this inner turmoil by blocking those inner feelings and bottling them up, will you?"

"Yes."

Percy considered his options and tried a different tack. "Do you fancy a pint?"

"Oh yes," gasped a relieved Cuthbert. The tea was left to stew.

Ronald and Henry were also discussing the effects of Nurse Brenda's actions upon the dynamics of the Valley. Henry expounded upon his natural leadership qualities that kept the status quo in place, whilst Marjorie rolled her eyes heavenwards at the thought of all the behind the scenes actions she had taken to avert the latest man-made crises over the years.

Ronald looked at his brother in utter astonishment. "You? Who uses his ex-mercenary skills to keep the Valley safe and under constant surveillance?"

"Not you," sniggered the pot-plant in the corner as Jasper joined the fray from his listening post.

Ronald snarled in Jasper's direction, "Not necessarily EX-mercenary short stuff. I could soon become current."

Jasper sneered in return, "Currant, eh? Would that make you the Scone Ranger?"

The Captain returned with fresh drinks and stood back as if to withhold them until someone paid him attention. He coughed. "I rather thought my military knowledge and experience as an officer and a gentleman held this Valley together, chaps."

Opinions were flying as self-worth battled with ego and delusions crashed against lack of evidence.

Arkle entered and stood surveying the scene. Good grief, she thought, that fabulous creature, the horse, was forced to wear a saddle and be steered by reins and a bit and yet this rabble was let loose completely unsupervised.

Her gentle cough went unnoticed, so she kicked a bar stool causing it to ricochet around the room and give the impression of being inside a pin-ball machine. The talking stopped.

"Have any of you numpties noticed that the Valley is being surrounded by a fence?" she asked in a dangerously calm voice.

Jaws opened and closed and the pot-plant in the corner gulped.

The bar suddenly filled with people all shouting about fences and wondering why the announcement wasn't causing the excitement they had expected.

Avril the local reporter was one of the last, because Constable Beecham had been stuck in the door and she couldn't get past him. "There's a fence, there's a fence," gasped Avril.

"We know," said the pot-plant. "Who do you think buys all our stolen goods?"

"Not that kind of fence," snapped Avril, wondering why she was talking to a plant. "It's going up all around the Valley."

Ronald sneered, "Late again, eh? Some reporter. It must be morning; I sometimes think that AM stands for Avril Missed it again."

Avril snapped, "Okay then, Rambo, why aren't you out there blowing it up?"

This was embarrassing and Ronald was forced to admit he couldn't until he bought some explosives back from the Valley mafia.

The sound in the bar rose to a cacophony, until Arkle sent another stool skittling around the walls. "Where are the idiots?" she asked.

"Right there," said the pot-plant, waving a leaf at the men's table.

"Not the usual suspects," sighed Arkle. "The undertaker and his apprentice." No response. "Laurel and Hardy," she tried; still, no response. "Oh, for goodness sake, Cuthbert and Percy."

"Yes?" asked Percy as they entered blinking at the sight of a full house and Belinda the barmaid's arms going like bee's wings to serve everyone.

56

Arkle glared at the late-comers. "Have you two twerps noticed the fence going up?"

Percy pushed his cap back on his head. "Oh, thank goodness, it's been on order for ages; that will keep my runner beans from escaping."

Arkle's face began to change colour and her fists were clenching. She saw the frown of concentration on Cuthbert's face and, surprising herself, asked, "Well, what are *you* thinking about, Cuthbert?"

Cuthbert had been watching the Captain struggle to bend and pick up a fallen beer mat. "Oh," he said, interrupting his own reverie. "I was just thinking that if we made the floors higher, we wouldn't have to bend so far to pick things up."

It was strange how quickly a gathering could break up in the Valley. Arkle's roar seemed to signal the end of the debate and the room cleared rapidly.

Chapter Nineteen

Cuthbert and Percy perched on a small hill and stared at the fence. No-one had even seen it being erected, yet it stretched for miles.

The Valley mafia were also nearby and several bushes and shrubs closed in on the unsuspecting duo.

Cuthbert wrinkled his nose and asked, "Don't you ever take your wellies off to stop them smelling?"

Percy sniffed. "I don't ask you about digging up your bodies now and again for the same reason," but he eased one welly off and placed it upside down on a handy bush at the side of him.

The bush promptly let out a gasp and rolled downhill, until it collided with the fence

"You okay, Jasper?" shouted Percy.

"Yes, thanks," said a voice from behind them.

Nurse Brenda looked on with interest as Oliver Ogden opened and closed his mouth like a stranded goldfish. He held the sheet of paper as far away as he possibly could as if distance would make the total smaller.

"How much?" he spluttered. "What fence? I never sanctioned this."

Nurse Brenda used the look she normally used for foreigners and recalcitrant males of all ages.

"I never sanctioned this," repeated Oliver with an almost defiant look in his eye.

"Oh, but you did," purred Brenda.

Oliver racked his brain. It wasn't wise to upset his nurses because one of them made his tea. A memory sparked and he clenched his fingers around the sheet of paper as if it was his permit to enter the management dining room.

"You said it was a Human Resources matter and if I didn't sign it the nurses would take offence," bleated Oliver.

Nurse Brenda smiled, "Actually it gave the nurses *permission* to take a fence from the builder's yard to the Valley, where our team of specialists erected it in record time."

58

Oliver scanned the paper again. "What specialists? Is there a separate wages bill?" he asked, going quite pale.

Nurse Brenda paused in the doorway and glanced back at him. "Oh, the Valley mafia prefers cash," she purred again.

Cuthbert and Percy made their way back to the farm and Percy broached the subject of Cuthbert's earlier depression as they walked.

"It's all right for a man of the world like you," Cuthbert began, causing Percy to glance around for someone nearby. "I've always had trouble with women," Cuthbert sighed. "My Mum was okay and Belinda the barmaid, but they were sort of duty-bound to listen to me. Then, along came Aunt Liza (shudder), Nurse Brenda and Avril the local reporter. Not to mention, the woman at the cattle market who misheard when I booked in an old cow to be sold."

Percy looked at his friend. *This needs an ancestor anecdote.* "Did I tell you about ..."

Percy was interrupted. He wasn't used to being interrupted. Well, he was, but he could usually see who it was and ignore them. This was different; even Cuthbert was looking around and he usually needed to be on fire before he paid attention.

"What's that?" they asked simultaneously as they made their way outside and tried to identify a strange strumming sound seemingly coming from all sides at once.

"It's the siren call," whispered Percy reverentially, and set off for the village with his head in the air like a cartoon kid in a gravy commercial.

Cuthbert followed him. Sometimes, he envied Percy and wished he could have a head full of facts and contradictions so, whatever happened, it would translate into an adventure. But he was Cuthbert and whenever an adventure smacked him in the mouth, it was usually just that - someone smacking him in the mouth.

Chapter Twenty

Ronald had entranced everyone in the Mandrake Arms with a riddle, but the arrival of Cuthbert and a very distracted Percy forced him to repeat it.

He glared at the pair and started again. "Where do players play in front of plays players?" He smirked and sat back to watch the confusion racing from face to face and back again like some virulent rash.

"Tennis courts," tried Belinda.

"Snooker room," suggested Henry.

"Cricket," shouted the Captain.

"Orchestra pit," said Cuthbert absently, still listening out for the strange sound.

There was a special silence reserved for one of Cuthbert's pronouncements and it descended now as Ronald turned puce with fury.

"What? Where? How? You of all people," he spluttered, staring at Cuthbert in amazement.

Cuthbert was suddenly aware of the attention and thought it was time to explain, even though he had no evidence of it ever working before.

"Well, we have players in my plays and they play before the players who play before them."

His audience gaped; Cuthbert had just out-thought them all.

Before anyone could say anything else, Percy whispered, "Can you hear it?"

"Hear what?" asked the Captain gruffly, still smarting because 'cricket' was usually the answer to everything.

"The siren song, it's calling me," whispered Percy again.

Ronald sneered, "I'm always calling you, but it makes no difference." He noticed everyone heading for the door wearing puzzled expressions, so he followed them.

Outside, everyone was muttering things like "It's beautiful" and "Never heard anything like it" and "Where's it coming from?" And, "Get off my foot!"

This last one was from Ronald who could hear music, smell horse and feel bones cracking. Luckily Arkle was entranced by the music and hadn't even noticed him.

They were all astonished by the power and poignancy of the sounds; some said it was like the wind through the boughs of a mighty oak, others thought it was the sea in its constant battle to rearrange the pebbles on a seashore; others the moaning of the wind bringing bad news through the telephone wires.

Cuthbert was actually getting sick of it; he thought it sounded like the tinnitus he acquired after a coffin lid slammed down on his head. He could have sworn he buried a smirking corpse that day.

Everyone seemed to be facing in a different direction as they listened and all were convinced they had pin-pointed the origin.

"That's surround sound, that is," said Percy in awe.

Cuthbert was puzzled. "Why would you surround a sound? It's not as if you can catch enough of them to make a tune."

This had to be solved and Ronald took charge because no one else ever did. He produced a pointer and marked out the Valley perimeter in the dust on the ground and split it into segments for each group to investigate. Each segment was lettered and numbered and each group was allocated their duties.

Just as everyone leant in to check their instructions, Arkle sneezed, obliterating the Valley pie-chart and all its letters and numbers.

Ronald began again and the same thing happened, just as he put the finishing touches to it. "Ar ..." he barked.

"Ar?" asked Arkle, putting more menace into one raised eyebrow than an Exocet missile could muster.

Ronald looked around desperately for help, but the music had swelled and everyone was miraculously looking everywhere but at him.

"Ar?" prompted Arkle, beginning to loom over Ronald.

"Ar (gulp), are you paying attention everyone?" Ronald gasped.

Arkle allowed the music to calm her and watched as the daft ex-mercenary handed out flares to the Valley mafia so they could spread out and fire one off as a signal to everyone else.

Arkle snorted, even her horse knew the mafia would empty the gunpowder out, sell it and give Ronald sticks of soil back later.

The mafia spread out in different directions, only to rendezvous at the back of Jasper's house for jam sandwiches until they felt like wandering back again.

Ronald lined up the rest of his volunteers who were volunteers because they hadn't been paying attention.

"You know," said Henry, interrupting his brother, "in this Valley we always seem to know the person who causes the chaos."

Everyone looked at Percy, who just shrugged because even he thought he was innocent this time.

People began moving out of line and checking for familiar faces and a cloud of powder went up from a compact as Mrs Biggle tried to phone the woman behind her to see if she was there.

Old acquaintances were being renewed and old animosities were being remembered until Marjorie asked, "Where's Elspeth?"

Elspeth had been getting out of the house and taking in some fresh air when she spotted the fence. It was a shock to a house-proud woman like her. It looked like a giant spider's web right around the Valley; this would call for reinforcements and more cleaning equipment than you could shake a feather duster at.

As she turned, Elspeth knocked over a fallen branch, which bumped against the taut wires of the fence causing a resonant ripple to travel in both directions.

"Ooh," said Elspeth, before setting off home for some very different equipment.

The Captain and Henry were nearing the fence now and the plan was to split up into different directions until they met someone from the next team, but neither liked being alone, so they used conversation as an anchor point and stayed together discussing past lives and adventures.

The Captain was saying, "I read about the scoop you filed from captivity some years ago, Henry. Dashed impressive - how did you do it?"

Henry paled at the memory. "Actually I relied upon Ronald to book me a room well away from the action because he spoke the language, but the twit didn't know the Hanoi Hilton was a prison. They thought I surrendered myself and had little value, so eventually they swapped me for a crate of whiskey and some cigarettes. What on earth is Elspeth doing?"

The men watched as Elspeth swayed with the music she was playing and Henry had to admit it was a virtuoso performance.

The bow was like a magic wand in her hands and her concentration was total. The only off-putting feature was being in a field watching a woman on a three-legged stool playing a fence.

The Captain had to fire three flares until he found one that worked - the others had already been 'soiled' - and people started to converge on the spot.

Elspeth had settled into a slow and hypnotic rhythm, so Henry sat on the ground beside her and asked about her new hobby.

"Oh, it isn't new," she replied. "I have played fences all over the world ever since my gap-year in Australia. The ones around the sheep farms were wonderful, because the sheep would scratch their backs on the wire and leave clumps of wool hanging there. This had a dampening effect and produced a really mournful sound. It was quite funny really, because the native Aborigines started painting lengths of tree trunk and miming to my music so they could sell them to tourists. The holidaymakers could never play them when they got home and assumed they didn't have the knack. We called them Didgeridoos as opposed to Didgerie-don't-buy-thems. My share of the profits paid for the next leg of my journey."

The music soared as Elspeth relived her youth in far-off lands.

Percy simply had to contribute. "We gardeners have mixed feelings about fences, of course. On the one hand they keep predators from the crops, but on the other hand it can be frustrating if you forget to put a gate in."

Everyone sat around being lulled by the soporific tones. Geraldine observed that the horizontal lines of the fence wire may have been the origin of the staves on written music.

Percy pressed on. "I have an amazing plan to make a fortune from bees, you know."

Cuthbert glanced across lazily and, forgetting himself, asked, "What is it?"

Percy shuffled. "I catch and breed as many honey bees as I can and train them to fly to the park in the next valley; then they bring all the nectar home to my hives and I live off the proceeds."

Cuthbert pointed out the obvious flaw when he said, "The valley park only opens from nine until four, Percy."

Percy shook his head at this lesser mortal. "Don't you worry about that, mate, I know where there's a hole in the fence."

Ronald was not to be out-done. "Fences are vital for security in my business too, you know. We were once put in charge of the prisons during a warder's strike and we decided to weed out the serious escapers, so we devised a quiz to trick them into revealing themselves. We asked one chap how high he could jump and he said 'Oh, about a metres' so we gave him a packet of cigarettes. The next chap in line answered, 'two metres' so we gave him two packets and so on. This went on until they reached nine meters and then we locked the rest of them up because the fence was eight metres high."

"They should have held the Olympics in there, Ronald," scoffed the Captain. "All those chaps able to jump nine metres, weren't you suspicious?"

Ronald looked slightly uncomfortable and admitted, "We were when all those at the start of the line stood on each other's shoulders and climbed over."

Elspeth suddenly stopped playing and stared at the hilltop nearby. There was a line of figures silhouetted against the sky.

"It's the Apaches" said Percy.

"It's the Zulus," offered the Captain.

"It's Nurse Brenda," hissed Cuthbert and watched with narrowed eyes as the figures seemed to glide downwards in formation until the matching bicycles skidded to a halt on the other side of the fence.

"Hello, Cuthbert," she said. "Keeping ourselves amused, are we?"

Henry stood and pointed at her. "You have no right to do this," he said in his best authoritarian journalist's voice. "We can contact Amnesty International and have you struck off."

Nurse Brenda considered this before she replied, "Yes, but you forget, we district nurses exist in that grey area between causing the problem and taking the blame. It doesn't matter who you contact, Amnesty, Red Cross, Green Crescent or Blue Moon, they have all read our report and no one wants to catch what you've got, whatever it is."

Henry spluttered, "All we've got is Twerp-inky-it-is," and pointed at Percy, "coupled with a vendetta against Cuthbert."

Several of the nurses gasped as a suspicion formed.

"Stand firm, girls," snapped Nurse Brenda. "At this stage of the illness they'll say anything. Remember Blackwater Fever and Bubonic Plague? There is a period of lucidity when all seems normal, but as soon as they are released, the infection spreads."

"Like Zombies?" asked a nurse; causing a collective gasp as well as the back-pedalling of several bicycles.

"Don't be ridiculous," snorted Henry. "Who believes in that sort of thing?"

"Well, actually," murmured the Captain.

"When you've seen what I've seen," added Ronald.

Brenda seized the moment. "See, girls, they've been in contact, all is revealed." And with that they swerved like a flock of starlings and rode away once more in formation.

"Well, that went rather well I thought," said Henry sarcastically.

Chapter Twenty-One

Cuthbert's table had witnessed many dilemmas, from the doomed King who tried to hide in its branches in winter when it was still a tree, right through to being case-hardened by blasts from the cooking range every time it missed Cuthbert during his erratic pacing.

The men were gathered there staring into mugs of turgid tea, either contemplating the future or trying to figure out the chemical formula of the concoction they were about drink.

Cuthbert was proud of his tea; people always seemed to admire it for ages before risking a sip. This was probably due to his skill in using anything spilled on the pantry shelves to bulk out the leaves when his supply was getting low.

Henry tapped the side of his cup with a spoon to gain attention, but the contents and the stresses proved too much and the cup collapsed, spreading a puddle that instantly soaked into the aged timbers. The table seemed to sigh at yet another indignity in its three-hundred year history. The spoon just sagged because no one ever noticed how a bent spoon occurred; they just put them back in the drawer and looked amazed the next time they saw it.

Looking around the table, Henry mentally totted up his resources, came up with nil, and asked for suggestions.

"Artillery barrage," said the Captain emphatically.

"Direct assault with Bangalore torpedoes," said Ronald as if playing Top Trumps.

"You'll need someone to repair any damage," said the pot plant in the corner Cuthbert didn't even know he had.

Henry expected the first two responses, but had to admit the pot plant handing him a business card surprised him.

"Anyone else - Percy?" he asked reluctantly.

After milking the attention for all it was worth, Percy came out with, "We still have the tractor with the mortar tubes, we could fire potatoes at it and at least we'll have a supply of chips if it stays standing."

Ronald broke the silence and addressed Percy directly. "You know, Percy, I have a really soft spot for you, mate."

Percy beamed. "Really?" he asked, sitting up straight.

"Oh, yes," replied Ronald, "it's a swamp just outside Rangoon."

Percy deflated.

Henry took control again. "Cuthbert, you have lived here all your life, there must be a secret tunnel running under the fence, surely?"

Cuthbert rifled through his collection of non-committal expressions while Percy muttered, "He won't know any, that's why they're secret."

That was it - Cuthbert was stung into action. It was his house, his table and his tunnels. He wasn't sure about the pot plant though. Jumping to his feet, Cuthbert went to the nearest wall and started tapping.

"Not that one," said Percy. "More to the left."

Cuthbert glared and deliberately moved to the right, tapping until he heard a click, and triumphantly pushed the panel as he walked forward.

He turned as Percy was saying, "Not that one," but Cuthbert was blinded by success and the dust from the coal cellar coming up to meet him rather rapidly.

Marjorie and the ladies were also having a meeting, but their secret location had settees, chairs and even curtains to pretend that the tunnels had windows. Margery had a map mounted on an easel and she pointed to relevant places with a laser pointer. The little red dot moved from place to place as the frustration mounted. Margery was saying, "This side of the Valley seems to have far less tunnels than anywhere else and none of them go under the fence. Geraldine checked any plans in the museum archive and Avril checked for smugglers' tales in the newspaper archives, and of course I've lived here all my life and I don't remember going that way at all. Nurse Brenda has fenced off all the entrances and exits that I know about, and dear Arkle pounded about on her horse for miles without falling into any holes. It doesn't make sense; there must be something we're missing."

Cuthbert picked himself up from the bottom of the ladder and dusted himself down to give himself time to recover and respond to the false enquiries after his health and the sniggers from above.

"Not feeling down, are we, Cuthbert?" asked Ronald.

"Nice manoeuvre, Cuthbert," chortled the Captain. "Not so dusty after all."

Percy was unusually quiet, but was still sulking and trying to nudge Ronald closer to the ladder.

Cuthbert gritted his teeth and looked around. The ladder didn't look too safe in the light from the room above, so he heaved a barrel out of the corner to stand on. Above the barrel and hanging on a nail was an old hurricane lamp, so he lit it and looked around. Waiting for the mirth from above to settle down he called out, "Anyone want to explore the secret tunnel then?"

The group gathered rather sheepishly around Cuthbert as he handed out more lamps and more and more embarrassed faces appeared as each one was lit.

This was Cuthbert's moment; he swelled with pride as he took his rightful place at the head of the line to lead his men, no longer a figure of fun, but a leader. Summoning his best rousing tone, he announced, "This is it, men, follow me," and promptly banged his head on the low ceiling.

"I'll lead, shall I?" sighed Henry, stooping slightly.

Cuthbert was vaguely aware of blurred figures moving past him and then his vision cleared and he took his rightful place at the back of the line.

This was another of the very old tunnels where an occasional mason's mark could be seen and the scratches of hand tools were everywhere. There is something eerie about disturbing a body of air that may not have been disturbed for centuries and they were all glad when Percy came up with a distraction.

Somehow managing to shuffle as he walked and keeping time with the metronomic slap of his willies, he asked, "Did I tell you about my ancestor who invented computer printing?"

Sensing, amongst the leaping shadows around him, everyone was interested, he continued, "He had been called in to decipher secret codes with a chap named Turing and he invented the first computer as a way of doing it; well, of course, you had to print out the results because filing cabinets have to be filled or they wouldn't be filing cabinets, would they? Anyway, as soon as the office juniors saw this printing device they started using it to print out hand prints and other body parts as a bit of a lark. All this messing about made everyone sloppy and they forgot to lock the door one night and this homeless chap with a long beard went to sleep on the cover protecting the printer. Accidentally pressing the start button, he caused a picture of himself to embed itself into the material. The flash scared him away and the only thing my ancestor found was the imprint; he showed it to his boss Mr Turing and because of the security lapse, they decided to never speak of it again. My ancestor flogged it to The Vatican where it became known as The Turing Shroud."

Percy wasn't sure about the impact of his tale because Henry had stopped and each of them bumped into the other.

"Do you hear that?" asked Henry.

The tunnels obviously distorted the sound, but the rising cadences and sudden staccato bursts were quite unusual. It was almost like women laughing underwater.

"Banshees," gasped Percy.

"Zombies," suggested the Captain.

Ronald moved forwar. "Stand back, chaps, this is my territory."

"I thought it was my farm," muttered Cuthbert petulantly.

Ronald flattened against the wall and sidled around a bend in the tunnel. Taking a deep breath, he rounded the corner and let out a death-defying martial arts yell, just as Avril launched her notebook in a flat-spin, hitting him straight between the eyes.

The men rounded the corner reluctantly only to find the Valley women sitting comfortably with tea-cups raised amidst gales of laughter and Ronald blindly lashing out at the invisible Ninja who bested him.

"What are you lot doing here?" asked Margery.

"Er, following a secret tunnel," said her husband.

"Does it look secret?" Margery asked. "Come and have some tea."

Cuthbert did a quick mental calculation before he remembered he was hopeless at it and hazarde, "Aren't we still on my farm?"

"Oh, Cuthbert," purred Margery, "next you'll be saying the attic in your farmhouse where we hold our knitting club belongs to you."

The Captain was impressed by the comfort the women had achieved and, moving to the corner, said, "Hah, you've even got a pot-plant just like Cuthbert's," and went to stroke its leaves.

"Ger-off," said Jasper.

The men perched uncomfortably where they could and tried to fit fat fingers into tiny cup handles. Ronald was just getting his sight back and looking for his unknown assailant, when a red spot appeared on his chest. He moved, it followed him, he moved again, it followed. "Sniper!" he yelled, doing a forward roll and checking all his pockets for weapons to retaliate with.

Jasper sniggered.

Percy put the laser pointer down his welly; he knew a source of fun when he saw it.

Leaving the women to their coffee morning, the men went further along the main tunnel in search of some sort of turn-off where they could surface on the other side of the fence.

As usual, they were accompanied by the slap-slap sound of Percy's wellies, except that Ronald was next to the last in line and when he turned around to snarl, Percy wasn't there. Trying to ignore a tapping sensation on his knee-cap, Ronald held his lamp higher and peered back the way they had come, but there was no sign of Percy. The tapping on his knee was now too much to ignore, so he looked down and gasped.

"What is it, Ronald?" shouted Henry. "Why are you lagging behind?"

"It's a duck," said Ronald sheepishly.

"What?" shouted Henry from the front.

"Duck!" yelled Ronald.

Everyone in front of Ronald dived to the floor knowing without question that when an ex-mercenary shouted 'duck' it was probably too late.

Henry kept his head down as a slap-slap sound came closer, so Percy must have survived. It stopped beside him and he felt something tap him on the head. Looking up caused his thoughts to scramble faster than a spitfire pilot. Ronald shouted duck, this was indeed a duck.

"What is it?" shouted the Captain.

"Duck," said Henry with a resigned sigh as the Captain ducked back down. This could go on for some time.

Ronald came to the front and joined the others studying their new companion. "Well, he's an improvement on the old one," he suggested. "Anyway, if he found his way in, there must be another entrance. He certainly didn't use Cuthbert's coal cellar, did he?"

The Captain looked distinctly unimpressed as he asked, "Well, what now?"

Ronald scratched his head before replying, "If we chase it away, it should lead us to the other way out."

Now it was the Captain's turn to scratch. "I don't think I've ever heard of a homing duck," he said. "What about you, Cuthbert … where's Cuthbert?"

Cuthbert was interrogating the women, or he thought he was. He had demanded to know how they knew more about his house than he did, and whether they had known about his coal cellar even he had forgotten about.

Margery waited patiently before saying, "Dear Cuthbert, you know when you men go on your missions to save the world and all the fainting women out there?"

Cuthbert nodded slowly as if trying to roll the memories to the front where he could see them.

"Well, all we can do is explore and dust and clean for when our heroes come home. That's how we know these things, isn't it, girls? But, of course, not even Elspeth could tackle that filthy cellar, even if there might be treasure stored in there."

Treasure? Now that was a word which always rolled to the front of the consciousness and Cuthbert could see it plainly. He even understood why the women were giggling; they wanted it for themselves.

Margery was saying, "That's why we put a barrel over the entrance, so that we wouldn't accidentally wander in and have to dust."

Cuthbert was already moving back in the direction of his cellar. Being referred to as a hero had stiffened his spine and he drew himself up to his full height, promptly banging his head on the ceiling again.

Percy meanwhile had been practicing with his new toy. The laser pen clipped to the top of his welly and he was trying out his quick-draw techniques.

First one way and then the other, placing the red dot first on one slab of stone and then on another, but he had swung around so many times in the darkness he had no idea where he was.

Putting the pointer back in his welly, he trailed one hand against the wall and set off in the dark until he collided with something that gave out a hearty clang. Touching cold metal, Percy wrapped his hand around it and discovered an iron pole like the ones holding up the fence.

That's it, he thought, someone had knocked a pole into the ground and come straight into tunnel. He'd done it; he would be the hero of the hour, because he could feel the tunnel carrying on behind the pole. Stooping to pick up a rock, he marked the ground with a cross so he could find it again and skipped back the way he came.

After many twists, turns and even a plaintive "help" he stumbled into a room even blacker than the unlit tunnels. An insane but rhythmic scraping sound filled the space and Percy shrieked when two floating eyeballs focused on him.

"About time," said Cuthbert. "Grab a shovel, there's treasure in here, Percy."

Now, put treasure and Percy in the same sentence and the effect is amazing, so think what happens when 'treasure' and 'Percy' are in the same room. Shovels scraped, bags were filled and the choking dust hung so thick it was like working in a blanket. The two dragged the last bags of coal into a side room and lay gasping for breath as the dust settled.

Sometime later, when the air was clear, the exhausted and dozing pair were awoken by the chatter of the women going past, leaping nimbly onto the barrel and climbing the ladder. Margery was last and she stood smiling down at them.

"Thank you, boys, that's cut ages off our journey," she said before disappearing up into Cuthbert's kitchen.

Percy was almost speechless, but being Percy he wasn't almost anything for long, "Treasure, treasure," he spluttered. "You took the word of the women? We've just done three months of housework for them."

Cuthbert waited for the spluttering to die down to a constant grumble, before he asked, "Is that a duck?"

The men followed the creature into Cuthbert's cellar as if it was quite normal to hire a duck as a guide.

"By Jove," exclaimed the Captain, "I see Elspeth found this place after all."

Cuthbert and Percy lay by the wall covered in coal dust looking like two smoke-blackened jelly-babies. All they could do was raise weary hands and watch the others climb the ladder.

Henry paused and smirked. "Got you with the old 'treasure in the cellar and where there's muck there's money' routine, did she?"

Two pairs of blood-shot eyes glared after him.

Henry, Ronald and the Captain had finished one cup of tea to the accompaniment of Cuthbert and Percy kicking the water pump and ranting at it and poured another as the slightly improved duo joined them.

"Well, we haven't achieved much today," said the Captain mournfully.

The others nodded, but Percy chimed in with, "Speak for yourselves, I discovered the pole."

Henry laughed. "I think you'll find that Amundsen beat you to it some time ago, Percy."

Percy glared and snapped, "Not that pole, the one holding the fence up and the tunnel that goes on beyond it."

Everyone sat up and paid attention. This was a real breakthrough. Everyone spoke at once and Percy sat back to enjoy the attention.

"Where is it?" asked Henry.

"Is it far?" demanded the Captain.

"Can you find it again?" asked Ronald suspiciously.

Percy glared at Ronald. "Of course I can find it again; I drew a cross on the floor."

The silence was that of a very noisy machine suddenly being switched off and the pause before it decided to start up again.

Henry leaned forward. "Let me get this straight, you found the pole?"

Percy nodded.

"You marked a cross on the ground?"

Percy nodded again.

"In the dark?" persisted Henry.

Percy nodded, but slowly this time.

Henry sighed. "Did you leave a trail of anything on the way out, pebbles, twigs, shattered hopes or broken dreams perhaps?"

The Captain interrupted, "Which direction was it in?"

Percy slowly pointed in two different directions with two different hands like a pair of broken compasses trying to find each other in the fog.

Henry and the Captain stood and took their leave; they had dared to raise their hopes in the land of Cuthbert and Percy, so only had themselves to blame.

Ronald shook his head at Percy. "You wouldn't have lasted five minutes in some of the situations I've been in, where men were tested to the limit of their endurance and beyond, and even then they went that extra mile."

"Wouldn't they have missed the target?" asked Cuthbert.

"What?" spluttered Ronald at the sudden hairpin bend in his narrative.

"Well," Cuthbert mused, "assuming their target was as far as they could have gone in the first place and they went an extra mile in the second place, wouldn't they have missed the first place?"

Ronald stared as Percy joined in with, "Of course, if it was a cliff top rendezvous, they would have ended up with a day at the beach."

Ignoring Cuthbert so as to lessen the chances of overload, Ronald pressed on, "The point is that a trained man would never have blundered about in the dark and come away dumber than when he went in."

Percy took up the challenge. "I've faced bigger dangers than you, mate. Have you ever handled Andy's snakes?"

Ronald sneered. "Do you mean the snakes of the Andes, you clot?"

Percy looked puzzled. "No, his name was definitely Andy. He lived in a council house."

Ronald stared at Percy.

Percy stared at Ronald.

Cuthbert had seen this before; they would go into some sort of trance where one would try to out-stare the other until one of them would forget what it was about and wander off.

He shook his head and went to do that flick of the wrist thing over the sink which was his version of washing the tea-cups.

Chapter Twenty-Two

Penelope Newton surreptitiously checked the medical records of the Valley residents. It didn't take long because there weren't any. It seemed, if you lived in the Valley and you were born there, you were appalled by the outside world and so you stayed there.

This Cuthbert chap took care of the burials, but he was so incompetent that the residents didn't bother dying.

The only Doctor the Valley ever had was a great lover of a stinking red-hot poultice that kept his waiting room clear.

Penelope didn't mind being known as 'Penelope Newgirl' - it was better than being labelled 'Newt' at nursing college. In a way, she supposed being given a nickname was a kind of acceptance, but this business with the Valley was bothering her.

None of the residents were showing any symptoms at all and the mention of a vendetta against Cuthbert seemed to rattle Nurse Brenda. Should she refer the case to the Department of Tropical Medicine or should she investigate herself?

Penelope cleared the desk and returned files to the cabinets before choosing the least squeaky bike and heading off alone to meet her destiny.

The women weren't too hopeful about the outcome of the men's foray against the fence and thus, after consulting with the pot-plant in the corner, they discussed alternatives.

All planning stopped abruptly as Percy appeared in the bar with spanners tucked into the top of his wellies. "Morning, ladies," he said as he headed for the cellar to tighten a leak on the barrel line.

"Is that wise?" asked Elspeth, nodding in Percy's direction.

Margery shrugged and replied, "With the Valley cut off from outside, he's all we've got for repair work, but don't worry, I've colour-coded the keg pipes, so if he tries anything I'll know."

The planning discussions continued until the pot-plant waved its fronds frantically. "Nurse Brenda," it hissed.

The women looked towards the door and were surprised to see not Nurse Brenda but the one they called Penelope Newgirl entering.

Margery made room at the table and replenished the glasses of orange juice, not forgetting to leave one in reach of the plant, which waved gratefully.

Penelope outlined her misgivings to Margery, Elspeth and Brenda and she in turn was filled in on all the gossip surrounding Cuthbert and Nurse Brenda. The air crackled with the energy of women bonding and the pot-plant took an instinctive pace backwards.

Penelope was now being given the potted histories of all the men in the Valley amongst much hilarity and Jasper was worrying about being trapped in a corner with them. Penelope had relaxed considerably; there was no chance men of that calibre could influence women of this calibre, so she felt on safe ground until the cellar door creaked open just over Margery's shoulder.

Percy appeared, stumbling slightly and with rings of several different colours around his mouth from sampling the colour-coded kegs.

Penelope stared, then she shrieked and then she ran for her bike.

Margery looked behind her and sighed. What was it about this Valley that made disasters breed and solutions run away?

The women continued chatting and the general consensus was that they hardly noticed being confined to the Valley. Most of the population grew their own vegetables and the pub's cellars were well stocked ... at least they were before Percy collapsed in the corner.

Mrs Biggle still had food on the shelves in the Post-Office labelled 'Only for use in nuclear emergency' and they could make their own social lives.

Geraldine laughed at the thought of this and had to elaborate when faced with curious stares.

Others had arrived and Avril the local reporter was sworn to secrecy.

Geraldine reminded them that she and Cuthbert had been quite close before she left to study archaeology, but the lack of social life in the Valley hadn't helped things.

"Didn't he ask you out, dear?" asked Elspeth, tutting at the lack of romance.

Geraldine considered this before explaining, as the undertaker, Cuthbert's contacts had been quite limited, in fact dead boring. Continuing with her theme, she related the time when Cuthbert invited her to an 'open mike' night, but at the last minute discovered it was an autopsy.

This was the cue for audience participation.

"Did they serve ribs?" asked Margery.

"Did they de-liver the invitations?" spluttered Avril.

"I bet the entrance fee was an arm and a leg," suggested Elspeth.

Jasper backed away and left by the rear exit, stepping on Percy on the way. This lot were making him *really* nervous.

Penelope set a furious pace back to the hospital and didn't hesitate when a security guard stepped out and raised his hand to stop her. Leaning right over, she peppered the hapless guard with gravel and skidded under the barrier only pausing to set the bike upright again and she powered towards the nurses' command centre.

Her colleagues stood watching from an upstairs window and Nurse Brenda smiled, took a sip of tea and remarked, "She's visited the Valley then?"

Penelope crashed into the room still holding the bike that had lost a tyre somewhere between entering the lifts and skidding along the corridors. "It's true!" she gasped. "All of it ... Percy ... coloured rings around his mouth ... staggering ... they keep him in the cellar."

The other nurses prised her fingers from the handlebars and sat her gently in front of a steaming cup of tea muttering the age old nurses incantation, "There, there, dear."

Brenda tried to hide a smile of satisfaction as she whispered into the phone. Outside a siren began to wail and automatic door locks clunked into place. The preparations had begun.

Chapter Twenty-Three

In the Mandrake Arms they heard the siren. "Is Elspeth playing the fence again?" asked Avril.

"No," replied Elspeth from beside her.

On the way to Cuthbert's farm, the Captain and Henry heard the mournful wail and turned to Ronald. "Are they looking for you again?" Henry asked his brother.

Ronald shrugged, but allowed the cadences to ripple along his spine. Perhaps it was time for another obituary.

Cuthbert was checking the equipment in his outbuildings when the siren began. To a man of imagination it may have conjured up visions of the hordes of hell intent upon finding the undertaker who had mixed up their names and planted sprouts over their plots, but Cuthbert had no imagination so he saved himself a headache.

Percy meanwhile decided to redeem himself in the eyes of the others. He crawled out of the Mandrake Arms and went in search of the lost pole. After stumbling along walls and tripping over his own feet, he pulled himself forward and reached out, only to wrap his hand around something rigid and cold. He had found it. He took out a spanner from his welly and proceeded to bang on the pipe until the others heard and came to find him, but the sound was nothing like the one Percy expected.

The cow hadn't been expecting it either and was having none of it. The other back leg launched Percy back the way he came until he slithered to a halt on the wet grass and began to snore.

The hospital had rehearsed the procedures endlessly, isolation wards had been established and all the top medical staff had hurriedly booked their holidays, so as to be as far away as possible.

Penelope Newgirl was showing real promise as a newly converted Valley sceptic and her newfound zeal almost matched that of Nurse Brenda. This brought Brenda's promotional instincts into play and she promised herself she would keep an eye on the ambitious young minx.

Henry, Ronald and the Captain found Percy, turned around and dumped him at a table in the Mandrake Arms.

The trip to Cuthbert's would have to wait, or maybe not, as they discovered him already sitting there waiting for them. Cuthbert would never admit it, but the eerie wailing of the siren had unsettled him and he came looking for company. He didn't believe in ghosts because he had convinced himself they didn't believe in him, but either way, he was glad to see relatively friendly faces.

Percy sat muttering to himself and Margery tutted as she fussed around bathing a lump on his forehead. "What have you done, Ronald?" she demanded, knowing the peace between these two was fragile at the best of times.

"He wouldn't look that good if I had done it," growled Ronald, wishing he hadn't when Margery flicked him with the bar towel.

Henry stepped in as the peacemaker before his wife started World War Three over a fake gardener with a trail of imaginary ancestors longer than Adam and Eve's. "We think it was a cow, dear," he said.

"Cowdear, what the blazes is a cowdear?" snapped his wife.

The men hesitated; they knew only too well what a cowed ear was and they were all exhibiting it now.

Percy distracted everyone with a moment of lucidity as he held an empty glass and pointed to the crowned standard mark on the rim. "Did you know," he slurred, "that every King checked that every glass had the same measure to ensure fair play?"

As innkeepers Henry and Margery felt duty bound to nod knowledgeably and Percy continued. "Apparently, it started with George the Thirst," and his head slumped down on his chest again.

Margery gawped at Percy as he started muttering again and shook her head. "A cow, you say, what makes you think that?"

"Well," risked the Captain, "the hoof-shaped lump on his head was our first clue and of course we were standing in a field at the time."

Margery looked from Percy to the Captain and back again. "This cow," she asked silkily. "Anyone know where we can find a bigger one?"

Cuthbert thought his hand had shot up to answer the question, but his brain did that strange thing where it lost the message and the arm stayed down. It had met Margery before.

Margery left the bar to find something interesting to erase the thoughts of methods of torture she could legally use on her clientele, and the men relaxed as they tried to ignore Percy's mumbling and occasional ramblings.

"Remember that rifle they invented to defeat those chaps with bows and arrows?" asked the Captain.

"Sharp," suggested Ronald absently.

The Captain snorted. "No, that's the bayonet, what's the point of having a sharp rifle?"

Cuthbert connected the words point and sharp, but his brain simply wouldn't let him take part, so he just watched as usual.

Ronald was indignant. "That was its name, you clot; it was the Sharp's rifle. It was a repeater."

"Why repeat it when you were wrong the first time?" parried the Captain.

Facts, figures and insults were flying faster than the bullets used to, until Henry returned from the window and announced, "Good time to be inside, chaps, it's foul out there."

Percy's head shot up and he demanded, "Who told you about chicken Monday?"

Panicked looks were exchanged as everyone looked for an exit.

The Brigadier noticed the flashing light on his desk phone and gingerly picked it up. He'd read the papers this morning and they weren't at war, so it should be safe to answer it. "Brigadier Superfluous here," he said, looking confusedly at the board on his desk and the plaque on his open door. "They've done it again," he snarled before snapping, "What do you want?"

Nurse Brenda purred down the phone at her end, "Now, Binky, just because they've swapped your name plaques again, there's no need to be rude."

The Brigadier's shoulders slumped. Only one person called him Binky and he only had one sister, so he narrowed things down rather quickly. "What do you want?"

Nurse Brenda's voice became official. "The operation we discussed, it's time to get on with it now."

The Brigadier panicked. "No! I can't, I hate hospitals and pain and blood, especially mine."

"Not your in-growing toe-nail, you ninny. The joint military operation where you invade the Valley, round up the inhabitants and deliver them to the hospital for me."

The Brigadier quaked. "That was a *real* plan?" he stammered. "I thought it was a parlour game."

Brenda sighed. "We discussed this; you even gave it a code name."

"I did?" asked the hapless Brigadier, desperately pressing buttons on his phone in the hope of someone coming in and interrupting.

Nurse Brenda continued remorselessly. "We need the men, the transport and perhaps even a few tanks."

Brenda held the phone away as he shouted, "Tanks, tanks, the last time we took any tanks out, the Valley mafia directed the first one over a cliff and all the others followed like lemmings. The beach looked like the place where turtles go to die and the men couldn't tell up from down for days."

Brenda waited for him to calm down before reminding him about all the free treatment the nurses had provided after the 'tank incident' so that it stayed their little secret, and then she listed several other little secrets they shared.

"All right, all right," he snapped as he hung up on her. Stabbing away at the buttons, he finally got one of them to light up. He took a deep breath and demanded, "Get me the SAS."

Olivia Tooting took the call from the Brigadier. She was proud of her job with the regiment. She had top secret clearance and was surrounded by terribly fit young men and some very dishy young officers. Some of them disappeared for weeks at a time and then came back with suntans and extra skills in riding motorbikes in the sand and servicing camels in the snow or something like that -they were very secretive.

A particularly dashing officer took the phone from her and identified himself to the Brigadier, before going very pale and looking around desperately. He politely asked for the date of the expected operation and jotted it down before saying, "If anyone can accomplish it we can, sir, goodbye."

Then to Olivia's amazement he ran down the main corridor banging on doors shouting, "Saddle up, get your gear, we leave tonight."

Olivia glanced down at the date he had written. *Strange,* she thought, *if they all leave now they will miss this new operation.*

She had no idea the reason for all the security she passed through in a morning was because the regiment had stolen several tactics from the Valley mafia and the mafia knew where they lived.

Percy seemed to have recovered somewhat, but everyone agreed it was really hard to tell and yet there he was in his turned-down wellies banging a spanner on random fence poles, so that Cuthbert could stand in the tunnels and listen for an echo, dash to it and bang back from below.

Unfortunately Cuthbert had been spooked by standing in a clean coal cellar, because its purpose had been lost and it was now just a hole in-between four walls, so he was actually standing with the others watching Percy tour the Valley perimeter making both noises and a fool of himself.

"You know," mused the Captain, "I really should fetch Elspeth and her violin bow. Percy's percussion section might come in handy."

Henry smiled and waited for a sarcastic remark from Ronald, but when he looked around his brother was pacing about and muttering to himself.

"Are you okay, Ronald?" he called. "Have you caught something from Percy?"

Ronald stopped pacing and stared at the sky. "That's where they'll come from," he announced. "Halo."

Henry laughed. "Halo to you too, brother." He added, "There won't be many of those handed out in this Valley, eh, Cuthbert?"

Cuthbert waited to see whether his brain was going to participate and found himself saying, "My dad always said we were lucky not to live amongst too many saints and not enough sinners."

"Why?" asked Henry, puzzled.

"Because the ones with halos would need longer coffins and they would moan about the extra cost, so we would have to charge everyone the same and the ones without halos would complain they weren't getting as much wood as the ones with halos," said Cuthbert as if what he was saying was perfectly reasonable.

Henry met his gaze and asked, "Were you close to your Dad, Cuthbert?"

Cuthbert thought for a second. "Only when I accidentally shot him."

Henry went over to Ronald and prompted, "Halo?"

Ronald tore himself away from his calculations and replied, "High Altitude, Low Opening parachute technique. They'll drop out of a plane miles away from where we could hear them and float silently over the fence when they come to get us."

Henry shook his head. "And what will they do with us when they've 'got' us?"

Ronald gritted his teeth and murmured, "Take us to a secret facility where we will disappear to be interrogated and kept in quarantine and no-one will ever know."

"We would know," hazarded Cuthbert.

"The parachutists will know," said Henry.

"The chaps at the secret facility will know," added the Captain.

"The interrogators will know," suggested triple M, having given up bird watching whilst Percy was making that awful racket.

Ronald waved his arms about. "Shut up, you dozy lot, it's a secret facility run by people who keep secrets at a secret location."

"Where is it then?" asked the Captain.

"I don't know," spluttered Ronald.

"So to recap," suggested Henry, "we don't know who they are, where they are, when they're coming, or where we're going?"

"Well, yes," admitted Ronald reluctantly.

The Captain turned to Henry and said, "Well, I don't think we have much to worry about, do you?" and they both smirked.

Ronald mentally shelved his plans for sharpened wooden stakes set at angles and trip-wires rigged to explosives and turned with the others as they realised Percy had stopped banging.

He had actually found the pole when it gave off a dull thud and he waggled it about shouting, "I've found it," just before disappearing down a hole in the loose soil he had created.

As everyone focused on the spot where Percy should have been, Ronald was heard to whisper, "He's gone; I knew it, now it begins."

Percy was in a hole, but it was pretty much his permanent state, so he didn't panic. "Cuthbert!" he shouted. There was no reply and his shoulders sagged. Why wasn't anyone ever where they were supposed to be?

He remembered one of his ancestors was supposed to erect signs at Rorke's Drift warning of 'Danger, Approaching Zulu hordes'. It wasn't his fault when the signs came too late, was it?

Then there was another ancestor who told Oliver Cromwell about a chap stuck up a tree thinking he would send for the fire brigade. How was he supposed to know it was King Charles?

He sighed at the misfortunes visited upon his family over the years. At this rate, given the chance, someone would blame them for planting the apple tree in the Garden of Eden.

He moved slowly along the tunnel in the blackness alone with his dark thoughts. Everything was Cuthbert's fault because he was bringing the candles.

After bumping into every unseen obstruction known to man, Percy stopped and rummaged in his wellies. He was usually prepared for emergencies and a box of matches rattled reassuringly. Now he needed something to ignite and burn slowly enough for him to find his way out.

He had once demonstrated a survival technique where burning a wax crayon gave off light for ages, but unfortunately they were in a tent at the time and he was never invited back. This thought led him to the rubber of his wellies and the idea of illuminating his own footsteps was a typical sample of Percy ingenuity.

Now he needed something to lay a trail so he could find the post again. This would be a major sacrifice because all he had was his seed collection.

Transferring the seeds from his welly to his pocket, he patted them fondly before applying a match to each welly and taking comfort from the warm, yellow glow around him. The smell was odd, but it was probably stale air.

Moving off, Percy was aware of the slap of his wellies echoing from the walls and if he hadn't known better, he would have thought he was being followed. He began to lay his trail of seeds.

Chapter Twenty-Four

Elspeth poured a fresh round of tea for the ladies and a mug for Arkle - tiny cups and make-believe handles just weren't her thing.

Margery looked around her circle of friends and relaxed. This time away from the men was important to them all because love and exasperation could only exist side by side for so long before mass murder occurred.

Avril relaxed from her long day as a local reporter trying desperately to find something to report and Elspeth had a respite from dusting because, well, you expected dust in a tunnel, didn't you?

Geraldine never understood her fixation with dust because as an archaeologist everything she touched was dusty anyway and, as for Arkle, most things crumbled in her grip so she never gave it a thought.

The ladies leaned back in contentment; this crossroads in the tunnels was pretty much ideal for them.

"What's that smell?" asked Elspeth.

Percy had discovered that his wellies did not burn at a fixed-rate like a candle or a wax crayon and began to speed up and leave some of the heat behind him. He was also worried about that echo, when he speeded up there was a delay before the slap-slap behind him also speeded up.

Flinging the seeds around so that they ricocheted from the walls, he accelerated again with the glow of burning rubber lighting his way, the smoke obscuring his vision and the echo propelling him forwards.

The ladies had all paused from the companionable silence and were comparing olfactory opinions, which said more about their lifestyles than they realised.

"Smells like burning toast," said Avril.

"Smells like a rotting mummy," contributed Geraldine.

"Over-heated horse," stated Arkle authoritatively, causing Margery to wonder whether she was referring to exercise or a microwave.

"Takes me back to my racing days at Brooklands," said Elspeth. "Definitely burning rubber."

At that moment Percy burst into their midst like an old steam locomotive leaving a tunnel. Surrounded by wreaths of black smoke, with flames around his feet and flailing his arms about as he distributed the last of his seeds. He began running around the circle of sofas and comfy chairs as he gasped and gurgled, until Arkle grabbed him and the ladies took it in turns to pour cups of tea down his wellies, whilst Arkle took the opportunity to pour one over his head.

He stood there dripping wet and smoking like a Red Setter after a bad experience.

"Don't worry, ladies," gasped Percy, "I've laid a trail so that we can find the exit." He waited for the murmur of adulation, but he noticed everyone was looking behind him.

"Is that a duck?" asked Avril.

Percy turned just in time to see the creature stretch its neck and swallow the last of his seeds.

Ronald was preparing for war. He had zigzagged all around the Valley to throw off any pursuit, and finally reached his weapons cache in a hidden cave in the side of a gulley.

Pausing to give the terrain a last methodical survey, he entered the gloom and switched on his torch. It was all there. The crates were stacked neatly and his explosives stash at the back was still covered in tarpaulin. Rubbing his hands together, Ronald set about prising the first lid off, and then peeled back the greaseproof paper to reveal his stash of … catapults.

Ronald rubbed his eyes and began tearing lids off and throwing boxes everywhere; it was the same story wherever he looked. High-tech precision weapons, all gone and replaced by forked wooden sticks with elastic attached.

He approached the tarpaulin with trepidation and a sudden memory of how impressive the fireworks display had been behind The Mandrake Arms. He had thought at the time that some of those rockets could have brought down an airliner. The tarpaulin slithered away like a snake sloughing off its skin to reveal … bicycles. New bicycles and old bicycles, in fact some of these could have been ridden by animals hurrying to catch the Ark.

Ronald giggled nervously as his reality was threatened. This Valley was stripping away his past; soon he would just be another, he gulped, Valley dweller.

Standing outside the cave, he roared, "Valley Mafia, I hate you and I will devise new tortures when I get hold of you, I swear by my ..." He reached into a pocket for his Ballistics Bible, but it was gone. Then he screamed, "And I will take you apart with my ..." and reached for his multi-tool, but it had gone too.

That's when he noticed bushes moving away from him and he sat down heavily.

The bush beside him asked, "Is the torch coming voluntarily?"

Ronald handed his torch over wearily and Jasper thanked him before going home for his tea.

The ladies had not been pleased to have their coffee and tea morning ruined and Percy was being made quite uncomfortable in the bar.

The rest of the men wouldn't have even known about his misadventure, if the women hadn't kept giving out bits of information like the steady drip of a Chinese water torture. He had to admit his still smouldering wellies attracted unwarranted attention.

"So that's where the duck went," observed Cuthbert.

"Did he eat all your seeds, Percy?" asked Henry.

"Are you sending him the bill?" sniggered the Captain.

Percy glared at Margery and observed that she was enjoying teasing him; she was smirking away as she lined up the handles on all the beer glasses behind the bar. Percy paused, he had never noticed before, but all the beer glass handles on the shelves pointed the same way. He waited until Margery had left and the men were deep in discussion, and sneaked behind the bar and turned one of the glasses in the middle of the row the other way, and then he sat down and waited.

Sure enough Margery came back, frowned and turned the glass back again.

Percy waited for the right moment and turned the whole lot the 'wrong' way round. Then he retook his seat and asked, "Did I tell you about my ancestor, the stonemason who built most of the castles on the English border with Wales?"

Everyone froze, but it was warm in here and they all had a fresh pint and for some reason Henry was keen to hear this one, so they all relaxed and paid attention.

Fact was, Henry had seen Percy turn all the handles around and after doing it himself accidentally once, he awaited the result with secret pleasure.

Percy shuffled and began, "Oh, yes, my ancestor was given the contract to build all the castles on the border. He sourced the stone and made sure the roofs were extra water tight."

"Why?" asked the Captain, puzzled.

Percy glanced at him pityingly as he replied, "It was Wales; they were concerned about leeks."

The Captain gaped and Percy continued, "He built every single one of them and they all came in on time and within budget. England was saved from a Welsh invasion."

"Was the King pleased?" asked Henry.

Percy's shoulders slumped. "Not really," he replied sadly. "The reason they came in under budget was because my ancestor pinched the stone from Hadrian's Wall and so the Scots invaded instead. Turns out the Welsh weren't all that bothered about invading anyway."

The Captain went into military strategy mode. "So why did we need all those extra castles?"

Percy shrugged. "So we could beat them at chess, I suppose."

Any further comments were interrupted by a sound like a knight in armour falling down a flight of stone stairs as Margery ran her hand along the rows of glasses crashing the handles back to the right place.

Percy stood to take his leave, but found his way blocked by Margery. "Now, how do you suppose all those handles turned the wrong way, Percy?" she asked quietly.

"Poltergeist?" suggested Percy.

Margery gaped at him.

"Perhaps I can help?" he suggested. "I have skills, I see dead people."

"So does Cuthbert," hissed Margery, "and he may be seeing *you* very soon, mate."

Percy gulped.

Chapter Twenty-Five

Brigadiers weren't used to being ignored. Well, this one was, but it suited his purposes. Most of the time in this man's army an order seemed to lead to an enquiry, which led to a court martial and someone ripping those shiny button things off your shoulders and telling you how much pension you weren't going to get.

He sighed, oh, for the old days when you could blame it on the horse or have your batman shot.

Stepping outside, he hailed a passing tank and insisted upon being given a lift to the SAS camp; they'd return his calls when he rolled up in this thing.

Standing proud in the turret and watching the long gun swinging from side to side in front of him, the Brigadier felt the whole armoured strength of the British Army wrapped around him. Unfortunately, when the wind changed, he also had the whole of the diesel fumes wrapping around him and every time the driver pulled a lever, the thing lurched either right or left making the most hideous noise.

"Stop, stop," he shouted, feeling quite queasy, but no one could hear him over the racket, so he shifted his feet and dropped down inside the tank, landing on the gunner's shoulders and causing him to twitch and fire the main gun.

The breech leapt back into the turret as if hungry for another shell and the crew froze, all trying to work out which way they were facing and where that particular high explosive shell might land.

The Brigadier grabbed a pair of binoculars and climbed back up, scanning the horizon until he saw a pall of smoke over the Valley.

Walking away with the cheery wave of an officer of the privileged class, he called over his shoulder, "Well done, man, no need for a report chaps, well done." And he disappeared around one of the buildings, leaving the crew to scratch their heads and wonder which excuse they could come up with this time to explain the missing shell. They would probably pinch one from another tank and let that crew figure it out.

Ronald and Henry had just met up with the Captain deep in conversation with Cuthbert and Percy about something that seemed to cause a lot of nodding. Apparently the Captain was describing strange burial methods he had seen in his travels abroad.

Personally, Percy had never seen any methods stranger than Cuthbert's.

As they headed for the Mandrake Arms like zombies homing in on fresh victims, they stopped in their tracks as a sound like an approaching express train roared across the sky towards them.

Actions and reactions were instinctive.

Ronald dived for the ditch, pulling his brother Henry with him.

The Captain leapt over the fence and was seen running on the spot due to a slippery cowpat.

Percy tried to burrow under the ground like a truffle hound and Cuthbert sent a message to his central nervous system, which ignored him completely, so he just stood there watching as the Post Office disappeared in a cloud of smoke.

He stuck his hand out and caught a singed envelope. After a moment, he called, "Henry, it's for you."

Everyone ran towards where the missing Post Office through a hail of confetti made from stamps and official forms burning like suicidal Chinese lanterns.

The women ran to the scene as well shouting for Mrs Biggle, who appeared from the smoke with singed hair and clutching something in her hand.

"How on earth did you survive that?" asked the Captain in awe.

Mrs Biggle flipped open her compact and replied, "I was outside trying to get a signal," and covered him in powder as she tried again.

No-one was happy indoors after that; things were serious and nowhere was safe.

"They really mean it, don't they?" asked Margery.

Everyone nodded glumly. Who would have thought Nurse Brenda would have so much influence?

Margery suddenly brightened as she asked, "She had a brother, didn't he join the army?"

The Brigadier started to relax; he had always found it was easy to put things behind you if you never let them get in front in the first place.

The camp seemed eerily quiet after the sound of the tank firing, so he stood up from his desk and stared across the parade ground. There was no-one in sight, but his office door slamming behind him was a clue to the fact he was no longer alone. He turned slowly.

"Ronald," gasped the Brigadier, "I thought you were dead."

Ronald smiled. "Everyone does."

The Brigadier sat back slowly at his desk. Ronald was privy to even more of his secrets than Brenda was, so this could get complicated. "What can I do for you?" he asked briskly, shuffling empty chocolate wrappers on his desk to simulate paperwork.

Ronald sneered, "Still keeping busy then, Binky? Remember that exercise you set up in Africa where we attacked the wrong village and we had to flatten the place and blame it on a stampede of elephants? The village elders were never convinced, you know."

The Brigadier blanched.

Ronald continued, "And do you remember that nice man who offered to store our ammunition for us so it wouldn't get wet and ended up firing it all back at us?"

The Brigadier shuffled nervously. "What do you want?" he muttered.

Ronald paused before asking, "Who has the most stories, do you think, Binky; me or Nurse Brenda?"

The Brigadier wracked his brains. His sister Brenda had stories going back to childhood, but Ronald had served with him at critical times and even worked undercover for him when he became a mercenary. His stories would be literally explosive.

Ronald decided that another prompt was in order. "Then of course there were the crates of diamonds that went missing. Live in a big house, do we, Binky?"

The Brigadier went into high-ranking splutter mode, taught at Sandhurst and designed to weaken the resolve of all lower ranks.

Ronald cut him off. "Save the bluster, Binky, it didn't work when you were *IN* charge and it won't work when you're *ON* a charge."

The Brigadier deflated. "What do you want?" he asked meekly.

Ronald smiled and slid a list of requirements across the desk whilst idly studying the pot plant in the corner of the office.

After Ronald had left the Brigadier sitting holding his head in both hands, Jasper detached himself from the plant, stamped his feet in front of the desk and shouted, "Yes sir, no sir, will do sir," and throwing a snappy salute wheeled into an about turn and marched away down the corridor.

The Brigadier absently returned the salute and thought he was rather short for a soldier and shouldn't he have been in uniform?

Ronald had walked over to the stores building, pausing along the way to greet various officers and men who said, "Ronald, I thought you were dead?" He was quite enjoying the attention, so he went around again. When he reached the stores building, the clerk gave him the usual dead-eyed stare and sucking in his breath said, "Can't do this lot, mate."

Ronald bristled. He had forgotten that 'store-keeper' actually meant 'gate-keeper' and obstruction ran through them like the letters in Blackpool rock.

Ronald growled, "Do you know who I am, *mate*?"

The storekeeper looked him up and down, which didn't take long, and said, "Oh yes, mate, I know exactly who you are, you're the chap who conned a young lieutenant into handing over fourteen parachutes and then sold them to make marquees for the church fete."

"Oh yeah," said Ronald, smiling at the memory, "whatever happened to him?"

The storekeeper paused before spitting, "I've been here ever since."

Ronald disguised his mirth and demanded the items be handed over - they should have been ready because the Brigadier had phoned ahead and here was the signed chit.

Now it was the storekeeper's turn to smile. "Oh, they were ready, *mate;* I gave them to your team to load onto the lorry. By the way, it's bad form to bring child labour into an army camp." And with that, he slammed down the roller shutter and insulated himself from Ronald's utter and incredibly loud disbelief.

Jasper had never driven anything this big before, but was confident it would make short work of the fence when he got back to the Valley.

He had only slowed down once after he hit a bump, dislodging a crate and sending a rocket howling back towards the camp. He was getting the hang of it now.

Ronald was storming around the camp looking for some transport to set off in hot pursuit when a screaming, fluttering sound triggered a memory and he ran towards the nearest bomb shelter. Unfortunately, due to modernisation of the forces and the fact that no-one had dropped a bomb on the camp for ages, the shelter was now a crèche and he found himself cowering from high explosives in a brightly coloured ball pool.

Emerging from the depths with ringing ears and dripping plastic balls as if his molecular structure was disintegrating, Ronald came face to face with a female Major holding two children by the hand.

"Ronald," she said, "I thought you were dead," and looked pointedly at one of the children.

He ran.

Chapter Twenty-Six

Elspeth had warmed up with a few scales and the fence was vibrating nicely, so now she could really get into the rhythm and express herself. The notes flowed and the hills were alive with the sound of ... a truck crashing through the fence, just as Elspeth reached her crescendo.

The Valley mafia clung on inside the back of the truck very aware of all the 'Danger Explosives' stencils on the crates, collectively wishing themselves back in the age of the catapult.

Percy had led Ronald through the tunnels after a fashion so he could get out and reach the army camp, and Ronald had laid a fluorescent dye trail when he was convinced the pole he had walked into was the right one.

Percy was now in the bar again with Cuthbert, Henry and the Captain. They were discussing outside help and only Percy seemed to know anyone outside the Valley, because Henry had lost contact with his journalist friends and Cuthbert simply didn't know anyone outside.

Henry prompted Percy, "So, do you know anyone of influence who could help?"

Cuthbert was dubious; he had started many conversations with Percy in his time and the omens were not good.

Percy shuffled. "Oh, yes," he began, "if you want outside specialists, I'm your man," and sat back contentedly.

Henry said, "Well?"

Percy straightened up and became alert. This was obviously serious and he was the only man for the job. "Right, if we need gardening equipment, there's Terry Cotter-Potts; if we need any woodwork doing, there's Chester Drawers, and for plumbing there's Ivor Wrench."

Henry waved his arms. "Stop, stop, Percy. We're in a desperate situation and I can't get a word of sense out of you."

Percy looked hurt. "Well, I'm a professional and most of my knowledge is secret," he stated flatly.

The Captain scoffed, "I can't see you keeping a secret, Percy."

Percy scowled. "Well, that's where you're wrong, mate. Gardeners are trusted with many secrets, or flowers and plants would die out because everybody would know where they were and pick them."

"All right," said Henry against his better judgement, "tell us a secret."

Percy ratcheted up the tension by pretending to think about it and then announced, "I bet none of you know about a rare wood used in expensive antique furniture that only grows in Scotland and can only be cut down on New Year's Day."

Henry sat up straight. "Big fan of antiques, you know, Percy. What's it called?"

"Mahogmanay," said Percy, heading for the door.

Ronald had commandeered a dispatch rider's motorbike and headed back to the Valley fish-tailing and sliding along the back trails. He grumbled to himself, but had to admit Jasper reminded him of himself when he was younger, except that he was taller, quicker and a damn sight better at hiding behind pot-plants than Ronald would ever be.

When he reached the Valley, he found the lorry parked in a depression between two hills, the tail-gate hung down and the back was empty. A surly member of the mafia stood guard alone and wore a Mickey Mouse watch with one hand missing pinned to his jacket.

Ronald sneered and walked right up to the lad using his most intimidating stare.

The mafia guard whispered into his lapel and Ronald guffawed, "You won't fool me with that old trick, sonny, there's no microphone in your lapel and the reinforcements aren't coming."

"I'm not talking to reinforcements, mister," came the calm reply. "I'm talking to my pet," and he inclined his head slightly to whisper something else.

Ronald's patience had always been like a veneer and now it was really worn thin. His arm shot out and he grabbed the guard's shirt front and watched in horror as a scorpion crawled onto his hand and headed along his arm.

"That's Elvis, that is," said the guard with a smile. "I was telling him he might have to whisper in your ear … ah, he must like you, mister, look how he's lifting his tail."

Ronald was appalled. He looked at the little monster and then at the scorpion. Sweat broke out on his forehead as he tried to recall his jungle training - should he use a stick so it would wrap itself around it? No, that was snakes. Push its jaws shut with his rifle butt? No, that was crocodiles. Shoot it before it tied his rifle barrel in a knot? No, that was Gorillas. The sweat poured, but the solutions didn't and the thing was getting closer. Ronald remembered the last tool in the Special Forces survival kit ... he fainted.

Jasper was impressed. Arkle had helped to unload the truck and position the rocket launchers on the hill-tops; she could even nudge them onto the right trajectory without resetting the computers.

The Valley residents began to gather and offer advice, without having the slightest scrap of knowledge.

Arkle slapped the Captain on the wrist just as he was about to launch a salvo at the dark side of the moon. "Don't touch," she snapped. "Leave this to the professionals." It made Jasper giggle.

The Captain was affronted. "How come you know so much about it, then?" He temporarily forgot the risks of challenging a man-mountain of tweed smelling of horse.

Arkle gave him a pitying look before replying, "I read Horse and Hound, you know, always plenty of self-defence tips for vulnerable gals like me."

The Captain was silent; the overload of images ranging from Arkle being vulnerable to 'gals' using anti-aircraft batteries for self-defence was overwhelming.

Ronald blustered his way to the front and started shouting about where to position everything, but he suddenly stared around spluttering, "What, where, who?"

Jasper sighed. "We didn't bring that old junk the storekeeper had earmarked for you. We had this lot from the ordnance testing bay - it sounded more exciting."

"But, but," said Ronald, sounding like a cold engine on a winter's morning. "They've got radioactive stickers on them." His finger shook as he pointed for the benefit of the others.

"Ooh," said Jasper, mentally doubling the price he could charge the lads in the next Valley.

Ronald was close to panic. He had been in some scrapes in his time and even seen the inside of a few jail cells, but this was the Military Police, they *liked* having guests and they even made cell visits. Ronald found that deeply suspicious. He was about to lunge for Jasper when he caught sight of the lad with the Elvis complex whispering and moving towards him. Ronald walked away, dragging his feet.

The storekeeper prepared for his afternoon nap. He pulled back the tarpaulin ready to use it as a blanket and stared. All that rusty old junk was still there. He thought he'd palmed it off on that obnoxious scallywag Ronald.

The kids must have loaded the wrong crates. He frantically ran around uncovering piles of equipment a military museum curator would have died for. All the stuff he had been stashing from the prying eyes of the inspectors was still here, so what had they taken? His eyes seemed to wander of their own accord and they focused upon a loose tarpaulin corner flapping idly in the draught. 'Over here, over here,' it seemed to say and the storekeeper gulped as he headed for the Weapons Testing bay.

Percy looked at the array of missiles and radar dishes in awe, but every time he moved to get closer, a member of the mafia stood in front of him. Eventually, when he paid attention, he realised they had thrown a human (well, mafia) cordon around him.

Cuthbert wandered over to the lorry and tried to figure out how anyone could climb up into something that high off the ground when he spotted a knotted rope hanging down. Leaping up, he clung on for dear life as his momentum turned him into a human pendulum.

The storekeeper paled. This was a disaster; it was even worse than the time he misplaced the tank borrowed for a charity event, when the 'Car-Crushing' went wrong as they used the wrong car park for it. He sighed. There was only one thing for it; this would have to be another careless cigarette end.

Luckily, he had been in charge of a unit of reserves here the day before with rubber guns learning how to shout 'Bang'. They would get the blame for leaving it smouldering. He took a deep draw on his cigarette, flicked it into the pile of crates and went to the medics to manufacture an alibi.

Chapter Twenty-Seven

Nurse Brenda stared across the desk at her brother. He had always been a shifty character and he was squirming now. She tapped an immaculately disinfected fingernail of regulation length on his desk top and asked, "What is it, Binky? You're hiding something."

The Brigadier was at a loss. Brenda knew all his childhood secrets and some of his adult ones, but Ronald had high hopes and low friends and that was a dangerous combination. He continued to squirm and hope that providence would come to his aid.

"Can I smell smoke?" asked Brenda.

With the missile batteries safely camouflaged, everyone wandered back to the village.

Mrs Biggle was still staring at the smoking crater where her Post Office used to be and the Valley mafia climbed into it and began erecting a structure from broken beams and tarpaulins, whilst the men stood on the rim shouting useless and contradictory instructions which were promptly ignored.

Mrs Biggle was touched. Perhaps the Valley mafia weren't such a bad lot after all, she thought, failing to see Jasper pocketing the rubber stamp used to endorse cheques and two other mafia members dragging her photocopier through what was left of the cellar and into the tunnels.

They even piled some crates and propped the wire grill up on top so she could spot Cuthbert pushing to the front of the queue.

Mrs Biggle wiped away a grateful tear and completely missed her safe following the photocopier into the tunnel.

The women meanwhile gathered tables and chairs together and were making tea for the workers and trying to decide what category the men would fit into. A voice behind them made everyone freeze into an involuntary tableau.

"Had some misfortune, have we?" asked Nurse Brenda.

Everyone turned and stared at the nurses lined up on their bicycles. They had obviously come through the hole in the fence left by Jasper's off-road delivery service.

Margery squared up to Nurse Brenda and snarled, "What gives you the right to do this, you could have killed someone."

Nurse Brenda was taken aback, but then she began to think on her feet. She knew an opportunity when it blew a hole in the road. "Well," she drawled, "you were warned about the seriousness of the epidemic and if you won't all come in to be quarantined, the military will take over and eliminate the threat by any means possible."

Even the nurses gasped at this; it was the first they had heard about it, but they could only watch as their world spiralled out of control and all sense of ethics were suspended for the greater good.

The women started to argue and the men began to demand to see someone higher up the chain than Nurse Brenda. The situation was getting quite heated and even Brenda realised they were outnumbered.

She was arguing in return, but it was hard to make herself heard … when the sound of synchronised bicycle bells drew everyone's attention. Brenda and the women followed the horrified gaze of the nurses and focused upon two approaching figures.

Everyone took a step back.

Stumbling towards them were obvious victims of this mystery plague and the signs weren't good at all.

Cuthbert staggered along, blue in the face, and Percy lurched behind him, falling, sliding and then clambering up before doing it again.

The nurses panicked and fled for the hole in the fence with Brenda close behind. She didn't fancy being left alone with this lot.

Avril scribbled furiously in her notebook in the realisation that her first longed-for scoop was probably also her last.

Margery managed to grab Cuthbert and unwind the knotted rope from around his neck, allowing the oxygen and colour to return to his face, whilst Arkle upended Percy and pulled the other end of the rope out of his welly where a knot had jammed under his foot.

"You twit," spluttered Cuthbert, "you could have strangled me, and why did you cut the rope?"

Percy snapped back, "Because you were spinning around and trussing yourself like a turkey, but don't thank me yet, mate, wait until your brain cells have all lined up again. It should happen sometime."

Margery stared at them and shook her head. "You've done it again, haven't you?" she asked in amazement.

"Done what?" asked Percy, looking around "Ooh look, Cuthbert, we got rid of the nurses."

Chapter Twenty-Eight

The Mandrake Arms was full again. The Valley seemed to be having a re-shuffle.

Cuthbert's kitchen was deserted and 'Whistle' had been seen sitting on the edge of Mrs Biggle's sunken Post Office, fishing.

Percy pointed out that the crater was just as dry as the reservoir, but Whistle simply smiled as he replied, "Whistle see, Percy, whistle see. All the fish from the reservoir must have gone somewhere, lad," and with that, the hood drooped as he concentrated on his task.

The Captain asked in a moment of curiosity and stupidity whether Percy's ancestors had built anything else after the Castles in Wales's fiasco.

Percy shuffled and his audience groaned. "Oh, yes," he replied eagerly. "My family were in great demand, so they branched out as architects. They soon had a reputation as being the cheapest and the best." He sat back smugly.

"Why the cheapest?" asked Ronald, "Were they still nicking the stone?"

Percy glared. "No, smart Alec, you didn't have to buy lino or carpets for our houses."

"Why ever not?" asked the Captain, impressed.

Percy leaned forward. "Because our plans were flawless."

On the next table, the women discussed how different their lives would have been if they had only turned left instead of right before they met the men at the other table.

Elspeth sighed. "I've always liked a man in uniform, you know, especially a fireman."

The others joined in the collective sigh.

"Me too," breathed Avril. "I used to try to save on taxi fares and stood outside the fire station for hours, but I never did get a fireman's lift."

The women sighed again.

Geraldine joined in with, "That's the problem with archaeology, all the interesting men are dead and you can't be sure you've dug the right one up anyway."

This didn't produce the same kind of sigh at all, so Margery volunteered, "I once spread a rumour in the offices that at every full moon I doubled in size." She paused for effect.

"What happened?" asked Elspeth and Avril together.

Margery sighed. "I was dismissed for 'growth myth' conduct."

After a pause Avril came in with, "That wasn't fair, are you sure it wasn't a mithtake?"

The gales of laughter from the women's table drew suspicious glances from the men who were convinced that all female laughter could only be at their expense, so they desperately tried to generate some laughter of their own.

There was silence, they were too busy listening-in to the other table; so Cuthbert saw his chance and rose to the occasion. "When I woke up this morning, it was like being on a real farm, it was surrounded by cows."

Henry glanced sideways. "Perhaps your house was in the way, did any of them sound their horns?"

Everyone laughed and once more Cuthbert was left wondering how it was he could feel adrift on dry land and alone whilst surrounded by people. It was a gift, he supposed.

Nurse Brenda was really quite excited; there was going to be a press conference and she was to liaise with the reporters and put the hospital in the best possible light. She mounted the steps to the podium and took a seat alongside Oliver Ogden, who skilfully moved his pad of paper slightly forward to show his superiority to the reporters.

"Who has any questions?" he asked, opening the floodgates.

Cameras whirred and flashes flashed and poor Oliver was soon overwhelmed. He was only supplying two words before he tried to answer another question with two more words.

Brenda banged the flat of her hand against the table. "You there at the back," she said clearly, indicating a mousy little thing whose only contribution had been to waddle a pencil for attention.

"Oh, er, um," said the reporter.

"Good question," boomed Brenda. "The answer is that we on the middle-tier of the hospital have the situation well in hand, regardless of the complexity of the logistics. In spite of the upper management, we are in a state of readiness and the outbreak has been contained."

The reporters scribbled furiously and their aversion to multi-tasking meant that Brenda could pick another dupe before a random question appeared.

Oliver was frantically analysing Brenda's opening salvo, because he wasn't sure he had come out of it very well, just as Brenda chose someone on the front row and sat back with a gasp.

"An excellent question," she said admiringly as the whole front row looked around to see where this apparent genius was sitting.

"Yes, you are quite right, there are others more qualified than we mere nurses, but we are the ones at the coal-face, we cut the mustard, we fly the flag and who is there when a sparrow falls?"

The reporters were agog. They had no idea all these skills were needed to be a district nurse; they scribbled even faster.

At the end of the session as the reporters filed out, they all stopped to shake Brenda's hand; some of the women even curtsied.

Oliver fumed.

The crow had spent a relaxing time gliding over the next few Valleys and catching up with old friends who didn't remember him because, let's face it, when you've seen one crow, you've pretty much seen them all.

He tipped one wing and glided over the new fence line. *Huh,* he thought, *if that's to keep me out, it is a waste of money.* He lowered his landing gear to land on a post and felt the gentle vibration of the wind through the wires.

The thought occurred, if humans weren't so dim, they could send messages like this. He tipped his head to one side and all the thoughts rolled together. Yes, he mused, it would stretch all around the known world and into the next valley like a line of inter-connected worms. That's it, he thought, it would be called the World Wide Worm.

His feathers fluffed with success, but the thought of worms took precedence and he went off in search of something to eat.

Oliver caught up with Brenda in the corridor and spluttered with indignation. "You hijacked the press conference," he ranted. "You made me seem ineffectual; I may as well not have been there."

Brenda gave him a long pityingly look, before replying, "Did they hear anything we didn't want them to hear?"

Oliver remained silent.

Brenda continued, "Are they any the wiser?"

Oliver shook his head miserably and wailed, "But that's my job and you are threatening it."

Brenda was appalled. "Nonsense," she replied indignantly, "I don't have time to sharpen pencils," and she stormed off.

Chapter Twenty-Nine

Back in the bar, the women had listed various duties utterly unrecognised by the men and wandered off to complete them. The men relaxed and the conversation turned to Ronald's adventures around the world freeing populations from tyranny and generally confusing any issue he became involved in.

He leaned forward. "You are the only people in the world who have heard some of my stories," he said proudly. "If you repeated them I would have to kill you."

"What with?" asked Percy.

Ronald's hand flashed to his underarm holster and came back empty, so it went quickly to his boot with the same effect. The next second found him writhing around on the floor ripping the leaves off a pot-plant.

"What on earth are you doing?" Margery asked as she came back in with Henry.

"I assume he thinks Jasper is in the pot-plant again," offered her husband.

Margery threw a dustpan and brush in Ronald's general direction and whispered to the other pot-plant, "Behave yourself, Jasper."

The pot-plant sniggered.

Ronald sat back down in a foul mood. "Where were we?"

"Knives," prompted Cuthbert absently.

"Daggers have a fascinating history, you know, chaps," said the Captain.

"Nah," said Percy, "load of old knives tales."

Ronald took the bait. "What do you know about knives?"

Percy rummaged in his welly and produced a small penknife.

Ronald collapsed with laughter. "What's that?" he roared. "Does it trim your nasal hairs?"

Percy waited patiently before he laid the penknife reverently on the table. "This knife, gentlemen, is responsible for the deaths of thousands."

All eyes focused on the insignificant object before them.

"How?" asked the Captain despite his misgivings.

Percy breathed, "This knife opened the letter responsible for the Wars of the Roses."

The room went still except for the surviving pot-plant, which stuck a straw in Ronald's drink whilst he was preoccupied and slurped quietly.

Percy elaborated. "My ancestor was a go-between who took messages from the Yorkshire faction to the Lancastrians and vice versa. They each wanted a symbol to put on their shields to identify themselves on the battlefield and strike fear into their enemies. One of them wanted the Thistle, but it was taken and another wanted a cactus, but nobody knew what one looked like, so my ancestor was given the mission to supply the emblems. Well, it was a hot day and he fell asleep behind a haystack, so at least it looked as if he had taken his quest seriously and travelled for miles."

Shrugging, Percy went on. "The best he could come up with was a couple of tatty white roses from the farmer's wife's garden, so he took those hoping the matter would resolve itself, and it did because he never noticed he had pricked his thumb on a thorn and one of the roses was now red. He galloped over to one of the sides and gave them the white rose and handed the other to the opposition. All the shields were then painted and everyone was happy until the white rose guys saw the blood-red roses on the shields and thought that it was more macho."

Percy glanced around. "The battle pretty much revolved around all these knights yelling 'We want *that* rose' and bashing seven bells out of each other. My ancestor was brought before the King to explain himself and accidentally trod on the original roses flattening them together. The king took this as a sign and the two sides joined together."

"And the letter?" prompted Henry.

Percy slumped. "That was a summons for parking his donkey on double yellow lines and the magistrate announced him as a man who held up a convoy. The King thought he said 'Envoy' and sent him off with the message and the other side sent him straight back and soon he was in full employment."

Chapter Thirty

Buses parked outside the hole in the fence with blacked-out windows. Two columns of armed soldiers formed a corridor from the fence to the vehicles and the atmosphere was tense.

The Brigadier stood in his open-topped command car and surveyed the scene. Some commanders in history needed to stand on a box to be seen, but his problem was banging his head on the top rail of a door frame. He began to suspect that lintels were designed by vengeful small people.

The situation had been discussed overnight in the Valley and the population came to the reluctant conclusion they could not risk another salvo from gunners who didn't even know where the stray shell went.

The village could be reduced to rubble o in the case of Cuthbert's farm, the creeping barrage might straighten a few walls and comb the thatch.

The Captain and Ronald had been vehemently against surrender, especially with the missile battery in place, but their confidence was knocked by an embarrassed cough from the pot-plant followed by Jasper's admission that the missiles they stole were dummies for display purposes and the only real one had been the one fired back towards the camp as they went over the bump.

The arrival of lines of Valley folk approaching the hole in the fence brought the two ranks of soldiers to a state of readiness and, as the women were coming through first, there were appreciative murmurs at the sight of Margery and Belinda followed by Avril and Geraldine.

Even Elspeth was not without her admirers and Mrs Biggle covered the first two in line with white powder as she tried to take a photo of them with her compact.

At a brisk command all eyes snapped to the front as Arkle appeared and both ranks took an involuntary step backwards.

The men were greeted in a variety of ways. Henry was recognised as the fearless war reporter he had always pretended to be and he lapped up the quotes from his broadcasts quoted back at him as he walked by.

Ronald advanced down the middle with his hands clasped in the air like a champion boxer as cries of "Ronald, we thought you were dead" came from all sides. Then he spotted the woman from the crèche who was also the Brigadier's female driver and she shouted, "Oi, I want a word with you."

He sprinted for the bus.

The Captain inspected the left-hand rank tut-tutting as he brushed imaginary specks of dust from lapels and peered down gun barrels. Only the sound of rifles being cocked stopped him going back down the other rank, and he climbed onto the bus.

Cuthbert attempted to ingratiate himself with the army because they got in so many scrapes - it might bring some custom his way. Unfortunately Cuthbert's smile wasn't used to public outings and the grimaces he produced were extremely unsettling.

Percy sauntered along down the ranks suddenly reaching into his welly and practicing his quick-draw with a turnip which made everybody nervous, until two huge squaddies picked him up and carried him with his little legs still cycling, before chucking him onto the bus.

No-one else was really of a rebellious nature and only Whistle drew any attention as he went past with his hood over his head and a fishing rod in his hand.

The Valley mafia clustered around the hole in the fence and were on the point of making a break back to the Valley when sections of earth and vegetation burst upwards behind them and men appeared from hides to completely block them off.

Jasper led his beaten troops along the lines of soldiers who patted them on the head and muttered things like "Chin up, lads, it will soon be over."

Some of the young lads seemed overcome and even accepted a hug from soldiers who had children themselves.

There wasn't a dry eye in the house until the Regimental Sergeant Major swept a metal detector over them and returned all the pick-pocketed items to his troops.

Chapter Thirty-One

The buses pulled up outside the hospital amidst a cordon of more troops and the sight of little old ladies being sent home to make way for the Valley folk.

Henry looked up at the two newly-built blocks with their multi-coloured panel fronts. "Let's get it over with, chaps. At least it's modern; we'll pretend we're on holiday."

They were met in reception by a group of people wearing protective clothing mumbling through masks.

After ushering their 'guests' into the special isolation section reserved for them, Oliver Ogden removed his mask and turned to Nurse Brenda and said, "Perhaps you should step inside and welcome them. You seem to be good with words these days."

Brenda sighed; wasn't this man ever going to take responsibility for anything? Stepping inside the glass doors, Brenda removed her mask and opened her mouth to speak as everyone turned to stare at her. "Right, you lot brought this all on yourselves, you know," she began, but the shock of hearing the security bolt slam shut behind her registered and she turned and made eye contact with Oliver, her boss.

Pressing a button on the wall-mounted intercom, she hissed, "What the devil are you doing?" in a voice dripping with menace.

Oliver removed his mask and gazed at her with a wide-eyed innocent expression. "But, Nurse Brenda, you've been exposed to them and what better way to report on the situation than to share their isolation?" Rubbing his hands together, he walked away.

Nurse Brenda turned slowly and gulped. She had never seen such a range of expressions all in one place before.

The reception room was full of Valley folk looking around them like children in a zoo and suddenly Percy simply could not take it anymore. He shook a set of double glass doors trying to get to the corridor beyond and yelled, "This is torture, all this great big hospital and they've locked an outdoorsman like me in a little glass room. Let me out."

Margery pressed a button on the wall, the doors whipped open and Percy was flung into the corridor beyond. "Oh," he said.

Various signs said 'Isolation cases this way' and red arrows were used to steer everyone into the lifts. When the Captain realised this, he muttered, "Waste of jet fuel that, why not just put a sign up?"

The lifts whisked them upwards to the top floors allocated to them.

The floors were labelled 'Male' and 'Female' and had interconnecting lifts, but the married couples promptly ignored this and everyone simply chose a nice view, all except Nurse Brenda, that is.

By the time she had risked associating with them, there was only a broom cupboard left. If she explored further, it would have been obvious the mafia had allocated themselves bedrooms, a conference room, a games room and a 'chill-out room,' which was actually the morgue.

Cuthbert and Percy had rooms next door to each other and Percy was appalled to discover there was only a shower. He didn't hold with showers, because they filled his wellies and made them overflow, putting his seed collection at risk.

Then he remembered he had sacrificed his collection to a marauding duck and this gave him a problem. Should he now start to shower or begin another collection? He set off in search of food.

Cuthbert was fascinated by his bed. It had loads of buttons and it could raise itself higher or tilt forward or back. He could almost set it to music, but it was a bit unpredictable and it folded up on him, so he tried to avoid it. If he had spotted the mafia member underneath it pushing the remote buttons, he might have figured it out.

Margery and Henry stood together admiring the view; it really was like a holiday for them, because the Valley could be a demanding place when you were convinced you pretty much ran the place. The truth was that no-one really had any influence at all.

Avril checked the phones to contact her editor direct from captivity and pass coded messages to appear in tomorrow's National editions, but she only got through once and he barked, "Hospital, I hope you don't expect maternity leave?" and hung up.

Geraldine knew no-one at the museum would miss her because, let's face it, they had mummies missing from Egypt for two thousand years and no-one had missed them yet.

Arkle was missing her horse and this bed was ridiculous. What was wrong with three bales of hay and a saddle? She tried once more to pummel it into shape.

The Captain and Elspeth settled in quite nicely, but her fingers began to twitch. There was no dust; she had checked everywhere - nothing. At this rate, she would have to start following Percy around.

Nurse Brenda sat and chewed her finger nails. She had been tricked and now she would be undermined and was probably being slandered and pilloried. It occurred to her, if she didn't know any of these words, she wouldn't be half as paranoid, but then she would have nothing to worry about. She carried on chewing.

Jasper sidled out onto the ledge until he sat beside Whistle. The hood was dipped in concentration and the rod was out in front of him with the hook way below in mid-air.

"You all right, Whistle?" asked Jasper.

The dry fisherman said, "Whistle never see the like of this again, young Jasper. My father 'Old Whistle' would be turning in his creel if he could see me trying to catch flying fish up here. He'd have asked 'what's wrong with the Valley fish, lad?'" Whistle nodded solemnly. "And he would have been right too. They don't fight back, they don't smell and you never have a heavy catch to carry home. Wise man, was Old Whistle."

The hood began to nod, so Jasper eased himself up and noticed the crowd collecting below. Waving his arms dramatically for effect, he climbed back in the window to find everyone watching TV.

The news announcer was intoning in his best doom-laden tones, "In a development at the on-going plague-containment area, the patients have apparently been trying to commit suicide out of desperation and a young lad was seen gallantly trying to talk someone off a ledge."

The camera suddenly focused upon a flustered Oliver pinned into a corner by reporters holding accusatory microphones inches from his face.

Nurse Brenda paused from trying to eat the hospital porridge and ran for the lifts.

Oliver was sweating profusely and pulling at his collar to the point where the press thought another outbreak had occurred, but even the plague was preferable to not having a story to file.

One of the women journalists was just demanding to speak to 'that lovely spokeswoman they met last time' when the sudden banging distracted everyone and they turned.

Nurse Brenda hammered on the locked glass doors with hospital porridge foaming at her lips trying to get to Oliver. Without the use of the intercom, she appeared deranged indeed.

Oliver seized the moment and took the credit for seeing the early symptoms in this martyr from his own staff. He assured everyone, by sacrificing one of his own, he had saved swathes of the population from being infected. With a last wink at an exhausted Nurse Brenda, he led the press pack away to cups of tea and cheap biscuits.

Upstairs, things became competitive. The mafia challenged the men, politely including Percy and Cuthbert, into a series of sporting events.

Wheelchairs screamed along corridors and squealed around corners at a pace to put the chariot races at the Coliseum to shame. The mafia won that one easily. Then it was the 'Curling' event where, instead of marble flat stones, chrome bedpans were skimmed down the corridor with a flick of the wrist to give them some spin. The men and the mafia were neck and neck in this one and whoops and yells filled the corridor.

Percy muscled to the front and hurled his offering, which wobbled frighteningly before tipping over.

"Just the empty ones, Percy," sighed Henry as they lost the event and something entirely different filled the corridor.

The women found a supply of felt-tips and were designing their ideal homes on the white boards in one of the lecture rooms. Most of them had en-suite bathrooms, walk in dressing rooms, a room for shoes and a shed outside for the men.

Arkle was happy with hers. It was basically a stable block, but she couldn't decide which stall would be hers.

Avril's house resembled a nerve centre at NASA with screens connected to all the major news channels. If there was ever a scoop out there, she was going to get it this time.

Geraldine began to recreate a famous museum for her to live in. Whilst she was surrounded by people in glass cases all day at work, somehow it seemed creepy at home, so she rubbed it out.

Elspeth designed hers like a bird-cage where, instead of vacuuming and cleaning, you just pulled a sheet of sandpaper out from under the floor every morning.

The men took a breather when they found somewhere they *could* breathe, and the mafia went exploring. They prised open doors and swarmed up lift shafts. It was like a giant adventure playground and every time someone saw them, there was a stampede in the opposite direction and the isolation zone was extended.

This is fun, thought Jasper.

Percy sulked; no matter how hard he tried, they always managed to blame him. Just because it usually was his fault was irrelevant; he slap-slapped along the corridors alone.

Cuthbert on the other hand became quite a star. He won the 'Sliding down the disabled ramps with a bed-pan on each foot' race and developed a technique where he ricocheted from one corner to another and mastered the ninety degree bend. He may have been slightly wary if he realised it was his lack of imagination responsible for his daredevil streak. The nightmares would soon tip him off though.

Percy found a room labelled 'Radiology' and fancying hearing some music, entered a room where he was greeted by a strange apparition wearing a lead-lined apron and a helmet with a thick glass shield and a badge similar to the one on Jasper's missiles.

The 'apparition' gave a shriek and a very ordinary man ran away as the lead-lined outfit crumpled to the floor behind him.

Percy stuck his arm into the space where the man had stood and saw the bones in his arm shown on a screen on the wall. "Ooh," said Percy.

Moving into the booth where his arm had been, he felt a warm glow and decided it was a sunlamp. He basked for a while before going down on the lift. *That sunlamp must be faulty,* he thought as a strange tremor ran through him.

The press pack was just leaving through the entrance and shaking hands with Oliver, when Percy shouted through the intercom, "Oi, mate you might need maintenance to look at that sunlamp of yours." He stopped as another tremor passed through him and the press were treated to a view of Percy's skeleton sizzling on the other side of the glass.

Cameras flashed like a summer storm as Percy struck several different poses for them and his skeleton came and went without any discernible pattern.

The press stampeded outside to be the first to write this new development, but the radiation had wiped every camera clean. There were no images, but undaunted, the press decided upon 'Ghost of First Victim Reveals his Haunt' and 'Hospital at fault; Should we send for the In-spectres?'

Oliver sat behind his desk and sobbed when he saw the first editions. "Go into medicine," insisted his mother, "get an ology after your name," and here he was, but it was looking increasingly like a 'Kidology' he had been awarded.

Percy went back upstairs and was fascinated by his reflection in the lift's mirror. Every time he felt a tremor, he turned into a skeleton with a hat on and even the voice announcing 'Third floor (Dong!)' began to sound nervous.

Nurse Brenda was gradually assimilated. The women could not bear to think of all the gossip she must be holding being untapped and unknown to them. She now ate with them in the communal dining room and in return she had given the mafia her swipe-card to gain entry to all floors and doors. It was like releasing a swarm of locusts with deep pockets.

Cuthbert was appalled, his worst enemy was now someone's best friend and he couldn't decide whether that made his friends his enemies or his friends the enemies of his friends. He went in search of Percy last been seen heading for the laboratories on the floor below.

Oliver tore his hair out as the press hounded him for more details.

"Is it true the zombies have taken over the whole of the North block?" asked one.

"How will the hospital decide whether they are the living dead or the dead living?" asked another.

Oliver snapped his pencil in two. "This all your fault," he retorted, waving an arm at the press pack surrounding his desk. "'Ghost reveals his haunt'," he spat, "and as for 'call in the in-spectre'."

The girl responsible tittered behind her notebook.

Oliver stood at his office window in the South block and pointed across at the edifice opposite. "There," he shouted, "see for yourselves, they are all contained and they are simply going about some everyday tasks we have set them to test reaction times and responses to evaluate their progress."

He must lose his temper more often, he thought. They were all crowding at the windows and studying the other block through telephoto lenses and he felt the pressure ease.

"Ooh-er," said one reporter, "Ddid you see that?"

"Where?" asked several voices at once.

"Top floor, third window from the left," came the reply.

"Are they dancing?" asked someone.

"Looks like they're beating someone to death," said someone else. "They've gone berserk."

Oliver snatched a telephoto lens and focused on the window. It certainly looked as if two adults were trying to thrash a young lad running for his life. He gulped. How was he supposed to know that Henry and the Captain were playing squash with meatballs from the food tray and a mafia member was their ball boy?

"High jinks," he blustered as someone else spotted something.

"Look at the floor below, five windows in, check the corridor," they said.

Cuthbert had just left the lift after arguing with the automatic voice announcing the floors and had found a hatch in the wall. He pulled it, then pushed it and then, breathless, simply leant on it and disappeared down the laundry chute.

"He's gone," gasped a reporter. "They've become invisible, they could be anywhere; they could be here amongst us."

The panic began to spread like rumours of a good investment and the result was about the same.

Everyone looked stupid, except for the lone figure still at the window.

The reporters filed back sheepishly and focused on the general direction of the man's lens. There was a collective gulp, then a double-take and then they fled.

They had witnessed the actual process when Percy invented the invisibility compound. They saw him pour a coloured liquid from one beaker to another and they saw the fumes spreading. Then he disappeared before their eyes, leaving only his hat and the two beakers in mid-air.

Tomorrow's headlines were writing themselves, because the reporters were too intent on their escape to spare any thoughts for word-play.

Percy sighed. This was his fourth attempt to make a decent coffee and the tremors weren't helping at all. Every time he shook the beaker overflowed and another piece of floor peeled back.

He reached for one of the interesting looking powders on the top shelf.

Nurse Brenda had pretty much been accepted now, especially since Cuthbert made himself scarce and confrontation had been avoided.

The panic-stricken press pack had been falling over each other all the way down the stairs and they now gasped for breath in the atrium linking the blocks, just as Cuthbert emerged from a huge laundry hamper wrapped in several long white sheets spreading his arms to steady himself.

The press resembled a real pack, one pursued by the hounds of hell.

Oliver lulled himself into a false sense of security until his secretary staggered in with the morning's papers.

"Oliver Ogden's Apocalypse," screamed one headline.

"All hope in North Block, gone South." screamed another.

"Zombies Rule - Ogden Fool" offered the next.

Oliver stood and faced the North block only to see Nurse Brenda staring back at him. The clash of wills met somewhere in the middle between the blocks, but Oliver was quite sure she couldn't get to him, so he reached for the phone.

Nurse Brenda turned her head slightly and said quietly, "It's time, Jasper."

Chapter Thirty-Two

The Brigadier left the Officer's Mess in pretty much the same state as he found it and changed direction when he heard his phone ringing. No good ever came from answering one of those things.

Olivia Tooting was also ignoring her phone, there was no point shouting "Red alert" down the corridor, because all the young SAS officers had deployed to trouble spots no one had reported yet.

Everyone in power or politics had altered the settings on their switchboards to 'Advancement and glory only' to vet out anything potentially career threatening.

Oliver stared at his phone in amazement as it purred harmlessly in his hand. His mother usually answered on the second ring. He felt abandoned.

The press had been ordered to stay on site and the atrium floor was littered with empty polystyrene coffee cups and discarded sleeping bags. It looked as if a colony of butterflies had experienced a caffeine-induced metamorphosis and had left the chrysalis cases behind, accidentally giving themselves a reputation as litter-bugs.

Henry was bored and could not resist the chance to relive his days as a journalist, so he was behind the glass doors chatting to the press pack.

Ronald was with him, because Henry could be indiscreet about some of the wars his brother had caused.

Henry held forth and reminded everyone he had been a well-known war correspondent and television presenter in his day. His words were met by blank looks and blank notebooks as they didn't even bother to scribble down his name and, with a sigh, he noticed how young they all were. He decided to up the ante.

"I was the top of my trade, you know. I was what you now call a 'News Anchor' and I came under fire from RPG's. Imagine that," he continued desperately, "an anchor being fired at."

Behind him Ronald snorted. "Waste of a good rocket, I would have aimed for the whole ship."

"And you are?" asked an eager young face.

Ronald paused. There were countries all over the world that thought he was dead and even more that wished he was, but it was the small percentage that realised he died rather regularly and conveniently that worried him.

"Oh, no-one," he assured the reporter, before making fake crackling noises and pretending that the intercom was broken.

Cuthbert managed to unwrap himself from the sheets and he rode the lifts. He had been doing so for hours because his worldly personality seemed to be compressed into this small space and the lift simply refused to register his presence and ignored all his commands. He wondered how long it would be before someone called the lift and set him free.

The mafia member on top of Cuthbert's lift lowered the roof hatch silently and giggled as he signalled up to the floor above him. The long canvas fire hose began to snake down the shaft towards him.

Percy had mixed everything with everything else in the laboratory and was no closer to the elusive recipe, so he decided to have a wander and see what other adventures awaited him.

Behind him the various compounds dripped into the peeling floor where they began to aggressively attack the girder work below.

Percy hummed away to himself and, as the lift door opened, he just managed to say, "Hey, Cuth ..." before they were both swept away down the corridors and around the bends in the stairs like a helter-skelter crossed with a log flume.

The reporters on the ground floor watched in amazement as the stair's door burst open and a wall of water climbed rapidly up the glass in front of them, only to recede quickly and reveal two very soggy patients slowly sliding down the pane.

One of the reporters scratched his head. "Wow, when this hospital evaluates reactions and responses, they don't mess about, do they?"

The others nodded in agreement.

Arkle had lost count of the amount of times she had changed channels on her TV looking for a horse-orientated show, and had given up. The world inside here just wasn't normal, she decided.

She even tried talking to Percy when he seemed sympathetic and told her about an ancestor who trained horses in Russia. She had been enthralled and asked why the venture had failed. Percy looked crest-fallen and replied, "They kept tripping up on the steppes."

Arkle growled to herself; she still hadn't caught him.

The ladies discovered to their delight that changes of clothing were provided and that local boutiques and fashion houses supplied them free of charge as long as the photographers in the other block caught a fleeting shot of their latest design sashaying along a corridor.

Dreams were coming true in this place - free clothing, sterile environment, food provided, and the men kept disappearing. What more could a girl want?

Actually there *was* more a girl could want. Nurse Brenda wanted revenge and then she wanted retribution coupled with revenge, and then there was always more revenge. She found a book entitled 'Operating without anaesthetic' and began to hone her skills.

The Captain found the Valley mafia rather interesting. It was like watching an ant hill and being able to understand what they said.

He noted a command structure and an unswerving loyalty to each other and even figured out how they were turning a profit after he saw two on the roof using rubber stethoscopes as catapults to fire stolen medical supplies down to some lads from the next valley. He was very proud of his military taught observational skills, and yet didn't seem to know *they* were watching *him*.

The birdwatcher and the fisherman decided to sit together on the roof after being dangled over the edge with accusations of being stool pigeons by the mafia.

When Malcolm tried to explain it wasn't a real bird, they offered to build him a glider out of bed sheets. They also promised to look after his binoculars while he tried it out.

Malcolm Masters with a Masters from Maastricht might be a human rights lawyer, but mafia rights seemed to be a world apart.

The ladies were having a great time and when shoes were added to the equation their world was complete.

Cuthbert and Percy slunk away from the silent sniggers of the press and carried on exploring. Cuthbert found an adjustable bed in the middle of a room with a huge sunlamp over it, so he lay down with the intention of having a nap and easing some of his bruises at the same time. He was soothed as the huge lamp came on, and the heat and light began to turn the inside of his eyelids red, but a metallic sound worried him and he opened his eyes to find Percy standing over him in a green cap and gown, wearing a mask and scraping two scalpels together.

Chapter Thirty-Three

Oliver Ogden was appalled. He leafed through a pile of paperwork and it was all bills for the incarceration of this supposed contagion, which, apart from some strange events, didn't seem to be spreading. It was time to justify himself, so he called a press conference.

The reporters duly filed into the room holding cups of free hospital coffee and packs of free hospital sandwiches.

Oliver focused on these things now and his subconscious attached a one pound sterling sign to everything he saw. He began. "I would like to announce there are definite signs of progress thanks to my innovative approach to treatment."

A reporter waved a sandwich for attention. *thirty-two pence,* thought Oliver.

Another raised his cup. *Sixty-five pence,* added Oliver, mentally setting off on the road to inventory.

"Was that where you dangle them upside down from the roof?"

Oliver was momentarily thrown. "What, pardon, roof?" he spluttered.

The reporter wearily checked his notebook. "We have witnessed several seemingly severe therapies, Mr Ogden. One, dangling patients from the roof. Two, flushing patients down the stairwells. Three, forcing females to parade up and down the corridors for hours. Four, allowing a patient to conduct experiments, without safety gear. Five, forcing a patient to recite nonsense about an imaginary career." The reporter snapped his notebook shut with a crisp sound of finality. "Would you care to explain any of this, Mr Ogden?"

Oliver looked around desperately as if there was a secret passage out of his office, but he had forgotten where it was, before giving in to his new compulsion and snapping, "No, leave my office right now and leave those sandwiches on my desk."

Jasper began to collect the items Nurse Brenda had requested; he didn't know what the plan was, but some of the stuff looked interesting and there should be a profit somewhere.

Cuthbert and Percy wandered further into the depths of the hospital and come across a room with stainless steel furniture and long sets of drawers set into the wall.

Percy slid each drawer out in turn and discovered they were all empty. Percy scratched his head. "What's the point of putting files in here? You can't reach the back."

Cuthbert came up behind him and said, "Look, someone has left a ten-pound note right at the back."

Percy scrambled in and Cuthbert slammed the drawer before leaving the room whistling. He would come back later, of course, but remembering which drawer it was might prove difficult.

The ladies watched TV. This was a real novelty for them after the Valley and its lack of electricity, because the only time they could be bitchy about someone's clothes was when a friend passed by your window, but here they had the whole world to watch and criticise, so they did.

Arkle wasn't really focusing on the clothing of celebrities; unless one of them wore a saddle, it wouldn't register with her.

She suddenly sat up as a new programme came on. "Isn't that this hospital?"

The programme change coincided with a meal delivery via the lifts and everyone retook their places chewing various unidentifiable delights. Gradually, they all settled back down and concentrated.

"That's you, Margery," squealed Geraldine as the camera zoomed in on a window showing a corridor with a very well turned out woman promenading.

She disappeared into a doorway and Belinda appeared dressed in a slinky number she earmarked for the 'Barmaid of the Year' awards.

This was great, they were TV stars. There was a hum of approval all round as Geraldine and Margery appeared together and linked arms, before throwing a coquettish glance towards the camera and exiting through another door.

The logo of the fashion house now appeared and a voice-over announced, "Our range of fashions is renowned across the globe and, as you can see, we cater for all you mature ladies out there."

There was silence as the word 'mature' silkily penetrated the ears, aggravated the neurons and exploded from several mouths at once.

"Did he say 'MATURE?'" came the collective gasp.

Avril giggled and risked, "Actually, I suppose I'm the youngest one here," but wisely didn't elaborate as all eyes turned to her.

"Someone send for Jasper," hissed Margery.

Cuthbert had been back twice, looking for Percy and now it was his turn to scratch his head.

All the drawers looked the same, but whichever one he opened was empty. Suddenly one of the top drawers popped open and a mass of red hair and a cap appeared.

"Hi, Cuth …" it shouted, before the drawer slammed shut again.

Cuthbert ran to open it, but another one at the other end popped open and he heard the same cry.

"Hi, Cuth …" before it too slammed shut.

Cuthbert found himself gasping for breath after trying to catch each drawer as it opened, and then he saw the janitor's bucket and brushes in the corner.

He set about industriously threading the brush handles through the drawer handles, until there was only one drawer left. He stepped back to admire his handiwork and bumped into Percy sitting on the stainless steel table swinging his legs reading from a cardboard folder.

"What, how?" gasped Cuthbert, digging deep into his opening remarks repertoire.

Percy looked amazed that Cuthbert was puzzled. He waved the cardboard covers and sheets of paper fell out. "Oldest escape trick in the book," he said with a grin. "They always send a cake with a file in it."

Revolution seemed to be in the air, but the men appeared to be immune. They were quite happy to be fed and watered at regular intervals and throw socks down a laundry chute. This was pretty much how men imagined life would be until women came along and complicated it.

Jasper now had another commission, this time from Margery. The trouble was, they had sold so much stuff to the other valley kids he would have to send some of his 'men' down the laundry chutes to buy some of it back.

Oliver tried to find a way to come out of this gracefully. All he had to do was lift the quarantine, invent a cure that couldn't stand the rigours of independent testing, and bribe Nurse Brenda to stay on-side.

Perhaps she'd like a new bike?

Chapter Thirty-Four

Penelope Newgirl was walking home alone when she sensed a presence behind her. She speeded up and then she slowed down, but so did her unseen companion.

This was it, this was why those Royal Marines had trained the nurses in self-defence, for when someone refused to take a pill or a ninety-six year old got a bit frisky.

She slipped into the shadows and crouched so as to minimise her outline, then she moderated her breathing and extended her arms into the 'fighting crane technique' and waited.

"Come on, missus," said Jasper from a nearby bush, "we haven't got all night."

Penelope felt somewhat ridiculous walking back to the hospital and talking strategy with a kid who had the reputation of a seasoned guerrilla fighter, but his instructions came from Nurse Brenda and they were colleagues.

Plasma was thicker than water.

Elspeth could see the change in her fellow guests of Her Majesty's Quarantine and knew something had to be done. The natives were about to revolt and Percy alone was revolting enough.

There was a series of classrooms on one of the floors and Elspeth appropriated a long black tutor's gown and then fashioned a strip of white linen used to wipe the chalk-boards into a cravat. It was a case of 'make do and mend' until she opened a cupboard and found a skeleton with a wig on.

At first she had thought it was Percy, but it was a proper barrister's wig and obviously the result of some forgotten student prank.

She settled it firmly onto her head and felt the power of the judicial system flow through her. Scooping up some random files and papers, she set off to round up an audience.

The press waiting in the foyer were bored. They had worn the spots off all the playing cards and couldn't afford to buy more from the mafia, so 'I-spy' was the thrill of the moment.

"I spy with my little eye," said someone wearily, "something beginning with 'B'."

"Trouble," said another voice.

"Don't be stupid," said the first voice. "That's not a 'B'. I thought you were a journalist?"

All eyes gradually turned to the glass doors where a genuine bewigged barrister stood before an array of women.

The intercom rattled, the barrister spoke. "Get me the head of Oliver Ogden."

Elspeth had meant to say, "Oliver Ogden, the head of the hospital," but the required menace somehow dictated itself.

Oliver Ogden raced down the stairs and then remembered the lifts, so he raced back up to use one and appear calm and collected when he arrived, but after all that rushing he looked like a chewed dog toy.

The legal profession always had this effect on him. They used words like scalpels and cut away a man's self-respect and then looked you up and down as if planning to take something else.

This barrister was already at the looking him up and down stage, before he even got his breath back.

"Are you the Oliver Ogden of the first part or of the second part?" asked Elspeth with a contemptuous curl of the lip.

Oliver, ever heedful of the press, tried, "Oh, I'm a man of many parts," to sniggers from the journalists.

The barrister paused long enough to freeze the flippancy and then said flatly, "Oh, you will be when I've done with you, young man."

Oliver froze. Every time someone called him young man, his life took a turn for the worse, and there had been the time …

"Are you paying attention?" snapped Elspeth, having to keep a tight rein on events, before anyone started thinking and spotted the chalk dribbling from her cravat and down her gown, and she suspected the skeleton had fleas too.

"Er, yes, ma'am, Oliver Ogden, ma'am, present and correct, ma'am." He was blathering and knew it, but a woman with a commanding presence who wasn't his mother was having a strange effect.

Elspeth consulted her imaginary case notes and asked quietly, "In your own words, would you tell me exactly why these people are incarcerated?"

Oliver looked around for Nurse Brenda for advice, but saw her on the wrong side of the glass smirking at him.

He shuffled his feet. "After acting upon a tip-off from a medical professional, we investigated rumours of a contagion in the Valley and, as a consequence, set up an isolation unit and moved the inhabitants here, for their own safety," he added quickly. He smiled; he could almost feel his mother patting him on the back.

The barrister gazed back at him through the glass and asked, "Would you care to name this medical professional for us, please?"

Oliver shrugged. "Of course, it was Nurse Brenda."

Elspeth turned and waved her arm dramatically and the women parted like the Red Sea to reveal Brenda standing there.

Is this Nurse Brenda?" asked Elspeth.

"Well, yes, of course it is," replied Oliver with a frown. "Why?"

"Why indeed?" purred the 'barrister'. "Why, we might ask ourselves, is she on this side of the glass when your whole argument rests on her shoulders and, indeed, so does your future career?"

Now Oliver could hear his mother tapping her foot; he gulped.

"She became infected, she had been in contact, she …"

"So had you, young man," interrupted Elspeth. "You were alone in your office with her and now you are amidst all those innocent, idealistic young professionals."

The press looked around to see who else had entered, but when it dawned on them they all took a step back from Oliver.

"No!" cried Oliver. "It's a trick, they're zombies; you saw the shrouded figure and the skeleton with a hat on."

One of the press accused, "You said we were imagining things, you said we needed to relax and eat free sandwiches."

"Coffee," screamed a woman. "What did he put in the coffee?" She held onto her throat and her eyes bulged, because that's how it was shown in the movies.

The press pack ran for the phones in an attempt to catch their editors before they became werewolves and could only howl at him.

Of course, that was okay for the guys from the Lunar Chronicle, but it was tough luck on the reporters from the Sun, and The Echo would be terribly confused.

Oliver gaped at the reporters as they fought for the telephones and then he turned back in time to see Elspeth scratching her head underneath the wig and dropping blank sheets of paper covered in chalk dust.

The whole recreation of the Old Bailey disappeared into the lifts and he was alone.

Chapter Thirty-Five

Oliver's secretary came in with the morning's papers and a glass of whatever effervescent tablets she had found in her desk. He wasn't a bad man, she thought, just hopelessly incompetent and useless at his job.

The papers landed on his desk and he could have sworn the legs buckled under the weight of bad news.

The first one announced, "Only quick thinking saved our reporters from becoming Oliver's (the axe-man's) next victims."

The next one had, "Sun Shines Light on Hospital Candle Scandal."

He really couldn't be bothered to work that one out, so he pushed the whole pile onto the floor, but he was still drawn to "Legal Eagle Represents Plague Victims - Ogden May Be Secret Carrier."

"Oh, great," he muttered, "try to save the Earth and you end up in six feet of it with a stake in your heart."

Cuthbert eventually found Percy again after they discovered a centrifuge and Cuthbert switched it on throwing Percy down the corridor for the third time, until he had stopped leaning on it.

Now Percy stood in the middle of the floor looking first up and then down.

Cuthbert followed his gaze and saw a spot on the ceiling that seemed to be dripping and a matching spot on the floor that seemed to be sinking.

"What is it?" asked Cuthbert.

Percy paused before saying, "I think I've left my coffee machine on."

Cuthbert thought for a moment and asked, "Where is it?"

Percy shuffled his feet and replied, "About four floors up."

Elspeth endured three showers and stamped on the wig repeatedly before throwing it off the balcony where it rested on a ledge and made a wonderful nest for a bird that wasn't too particular.

Penelope Newgirl had given Jasper a message for Nurse Brenda and went about her normal duties, watching and waiting for the call for action. She checked several cabinets for the documents Brenda had mentioned and then left a message where it would be delivered with the food.

Percy unpeeled the plastic covering from his apple crumble just as Cuthbert bent to pick something up off the floor. "Percy," he said, "there's something written under your plate."

Now Cuthbert and Percy were neck and neck in the 'you get me and I'll get you' stakes, but Percy thought this was too imaginative for Cuthbert, so he promptly dumped the steaming hot dessert in his own lap as he turned the plate over.

Cuthbert watched as his friend jumped around trying to make some fall into his wellies to eat later and then they read the message.

It said, "In south block, gone cold, not much hope now. Penelope."

It should have read 'trail gone cold,' but Percy's custard-coated fingers had smudged it.

Percy sprang to attention, a damsel in distress. The blood of his heroic ancestors pumped through his veins; this was more like it.

"Cold indeed," he laughed. "If I had been with Scott of the Antarctic," he said to Cuthbert, "he would have got home safely."

Cuthbert thought about it for a moment, before saying, "Scott of Southampton doesn't quite have the same ring to it though does it?"

Percy hadn't heard him. He was on a mission and he was headed for the service tunnel.

Chapter Thirty-Six

Oliver paced in his office; he sensed he was coming to the end of something, but exactly what eluded him? His patience; that was a yes; his tether; another yes; his career …

He gulped and dashed to another room where the photo-journalists still had their cameras trained on the other block. "Anything to report?" he asked pompously, as if anyone cared about him since he stopped the free coffee.

Most of the people in the room ignored him, but one man at the window muttered, "That's odd."

Oliver didn't like 'odd' - he preferred 'definite' or 'balanced' or his special favourite 'the success was all down to you, boss.' Actually, he was still waiting to hear that one.

He joined the man at the window and used a camera mounted on a tripod nearby, but everything looked the same to him.

"What's odd?" he asked.

The other man waved vaguely. "I could swear that the desks from that floor suddenly appeared on the floor below."

Oliver snorted. "Ridiculous, you've mixed up the floors."

Someone else asked hesitatingly, "Isn't that the floor where the skeleton in a hat was mixing chemicals?"

Oliver felt the breath of doom on the back of his neck.

Cuthbert had lost sight of Percy in the tunnel ahead, but saw a sudden throbbing green glow that soon faded again and he rushed to keep up.

He hadn't known about this tunnel, but from the direction of travel, it linked the blocks together and there were pipes and cables everywhere, just the sort of place Percy would find by instinct alone.

When he caught up with his friend, Percy was staring up at a huge hopper-fed boiler with a big clock-like pressure gauge on the front and a greasy rag had appeared in his hand. He was muttering to himself as he reiterated the message, "In South block, gone cold; not much hope now. Penelope."

He turned to Cuthbert. "No time to waste, mate, hoist me up on your shoulders, so that I can reach that valve."

Cuthbert would do anything for a friend, but as soon as Percy was on his shoulders, he realised just how close he was to his wellies and his odour-eaters were obviously on a diet again, so he tried to breathe through his ears.

A tremor ran through Percy and went to earth through Cuthbert. The walls glowed green and then faded again.

"Just a little more," gasped Percy, fetching a spanner from inside his welly and wedging it into the wheel valve. The wheel creaked in protest as Percy heaved down on it, before another tremor gave him superhuman strength and he turned the thing almost a full revolution before the green glow faded again.

Percy jumped off and the pair stepped back to admire Percy's handiwork. The needle on the gauge headed towards the red area at the top and Percy wiped his hands on his mechanic's rag.

"She won't be cold now, Cuthbert," he said. "I reckon we've saved the day again, mate."

The massive boiler gave a judder as the needle reached the red area and when it crossed fully into the red triangle, things began to happen.

A strange chugging sound emanated from all the pipes in the access tunnel and the boiler vibrated the floor to the point where Cuthbert's belated thoughts were almost catching up with his reactions.

Cuthbert stared at the jets of steam suddenly shooting out from various pipe-joints and heard the rivets pinging out of the seams before ricocheting along the tunnel.

"Uh-oh," said Percy.

Oliver felt the vibrations through the soles of his feet and they were getting stronger. The building was beginning to shake.

"What is it?" he asked wide-eyed.

One of the reporters attempted to pack away his expensive kit, but it kept vibrating along the floor away from him. "I've seen this before," he shouted over the rumbling. "A volcano erupted in Patagonia and we had to flee."

Another reporter asked, "Is there anything we can do?"

The first man shouted, "Well, they tried sacrificing a useless chicken."

All eyes turned to Oliver.

Percy hurtled along the tunnel and with them being modern and man-made, at least he could run faster than in the tunnels in the Valley, but even then he couldn't catch Cuthbert.

The journalists raced down the stairs, bouncing off corners and off each other as they went.

Oliver found enough breath to ask, "Did anyone survive the volcano?"

"How would I know?" gasped the journalist. "I got jet-lag running across the border."

The women gazed wistfully from the top floor windows and began to comment on all the activity in the car park. People were streaming out of the other block and gazing back up at it.

"Oh, dear," said Elspeth, "I think our block is getting taller."

The staff from the stricken block looked on in horror as all their personalised coffee mugs and biscuit supplies were mangled as the hospital collapsed.

The onrush of air burst through the atrium and blew the glass doors off the isolation block.

The Valley folk came out of the lifts just as Penelope Newgirl bumped into Percy.

"That was close," she said. "I was almost a goner."

"You're welcome," gasped Percy as two desks and a filing cabinet fell to earth behind them. Percy looked up through the hole and decided he would need to find another laboratory.

The inhabitants of the isolation block were more than happy to accommodate all the refugees.

Quite frankly, they were sick of seeing each other - at least in the Valley they could go home and have some peace ... until Margery appeared from a secret door or Elspeth wandered in and started dusting.

Oliver and Nurse Brenda circled each other and snarled whenever they were in the same room, but everyone else seemed to have forgotten why the Valley folk were even there.

Jasper was depressed, he never did find out what Nurse Brenda had been planning and he lost a fortune on selling the furniture from the other block. He even had to give the deposit back.

The lecture hall was now being used as a common room and Percy was in his element. He had even drawn his family tree on the huge screen behind him and was answering questions from eager young students.

"Can you really trace you ancestors back to biblical times?" asked an earnest young woman with a pony tail.

"Oh, yes," replied Percy eagerly as he slapped a wooden pointer against a name towards the top of the board. "This was Zebediah Plumm and he was an entrepreneur, even back then. He spent hours moulding little clay men with beards and long robes."

"Whatever for?" asked the girl.

Percy shrugged. "Just trying to make a prophet, I suppose."

Margery and Elspeth had taken a couple under their wing and found them a room. Their names were Harold and Marion, but when Margery realised how controlling the husband was pulling all the strings, she dubbed the wife, 'Marionette.'

Cuthbert had been looking at the hole in the floor where Percy's Barista career began and ended on pretty much the same day and it was only when he walked around the hole and couldn't get back that he realised it was getting bigger.

The Captain took over another lecture theatre and regaled some students with his tales of derring-do, but somehow the advice "If you take as long as you can to synchronise your watch, you can sometimes miss the whole battle," didn't quite seem to fit.

Henry was still smarting from not being recognised by those young oiks of journalists. Perhaps it was time for a new career? He didn't have the money to be an investment banker and his old school didn't get him far, because it had 'comprehensive' after it. Perhaps politics was the answer? Henry knew plenty of people who didn't know how they had got into it, or how to get out of it, but at least they had a pension.

As for Ronald, he kept a low profile after the reporters had asked who he was. He could move onto pastures new, but he didn't feel threatened here. He stretched out on the settee in the doctors' lounge behind the door he had camouflaged for complete privacy. Who was there to worry about here? Who could possibly harm him? Percy? He laughed, just as the ceiling collapsed and deposited several desks, filing cabinets and a water-cooler on him.

Oliver demanded his own office and telephone line in the surviving block and he had regretted it instantly as the phone never stopped ringing and his secretary knew where to bring the day's papers.

The latest drama had been exaggerated into "Assassination Attempt on Pillars of the Press." It sounded more like the Acropolis than this dump, he thought. The next one asked, "What Does Oliver Ogden Have to Hide Under the Rubble?" He sighed; this was nothing like the job he had expected. He imagined Doctors touching their forelocks and nurses curtseying in the corridors as he swept past.

At this rate, *he* would be sweeping as *they* went past.

The isolation block was actually getting quite crowded now, what with the influx of office workers from the ruins next door and the mysteriously disappearing floors above them.

Margery noticed that Cuthbert and Nurse Brenda were being forced into closer proximity by the lack of space, but they were still eyeing each other warily.

Sidling up to Cuthbert, she asked, "Are you and Nurse Brenda going to call a truce then? It would make life a lot easier for us all, you know."

Cuthbert blinked once, then twice before seeming to pull himself together as Margery took a nervous step back.

"Are you all right?" she asked, suddenly realising who this was and the possible scope of the reply.

"Oh, yes," said Cuthbert warily as he cast a glance at his arch-enemy Brenda. "I have a plan," he confided.

Margery sighed. "And the plan is?"

Cuthbert stepped closer and whispered, "I'm learning to blink in Morse code, so I can tell the paramedics that Nurse Brenda did it." And with an unintelligible flicking of his eyelids, he was off.

Margery sighed again.

Percy had attracted quite a student following after his lectures and they tended to trail him. As he passed through a creaking door, he pulled a screwdriver out of his welly and tightened the hinge; there was an admiring gasp from his fans.

Percy bowed in acknowledgement and explained, "It's something I picked up as a mechanic at Sea-World. I had a tool for every porpoise; I was even presented with a diamond-encrusted spanner, but I had to sell it; that was a real wrench."

The mafia meanwhile contented themselves with salvaging items from the wreckage next door and selling things back to their owners.

If anyone complained, Jasper would point to Arkle mooching about and throwing desks around out of boredom. He would explain she was their 'complaints department'.

Percy returned to the lecture room and his students were seated before him as he swung his little legs under the desk. He gave them a lecture about his ancestors including, Isambard Kingdom Plumm, the social worker who built bridges between communities; then there was Robert Stevenson-Plumm, who stopped the locals from going off the rails, or he would give them a rocket. Engineering, he explained, was in the blood of the Plumm family.

"Iron-rich diet, eh?" asked a voice similar to Cuthbert's, but lost in the crowd.

Percy glared, but continued, "The biggest enemy of the engineer," he explained, "is the sign-writer."

"As in, 'may contain nuts'?" asked that voice again.

Percy glared again, but he had insisted upon the spotlights being trained on him and felt like one of the Dambusters caught in the glare. He continued, "Walk into any of these giant hardware stores and behold."

He stood up from his desk and began to pace, he raised his arms as a messianic fervour gripped him and his voice thundered, "Why do they proclaim that 'Stainless Steel Sinks'?" He roared, "We engineers already know that!"

He pointed into the crowd and hissed, "And lo, as ye venture into the sale department, they will tempt you with dimmer switches disguised as 'reduced lighting'." His finger shook as he proclaimed, "Beware, the sign-writers, they entice us into a fencing department where they don't sell swords, they promise Plant-Hire and instead surround you with tractors and they confuse the cheese-makers with signs saying 'Whey In' and 'Whey Out'."

Percy turned his back on his acolytes and took a deep breath as he prepared for his clinching argument.

The students were enthralled. All thoughts of medicine had disappeared; they were going to be *engineers.*

The familiar voice from the back asked calmly, "Do they provide an oily rag?"

The students glanced at each other.

The voice came again. "And that big heavy bag of tools?"

The students gulped.

"Do the black nails, bad backs and bad knees come straight away or do they come in instalments?" the voice insisted.

Stethoscopes appeared out of the pockets of pristine white coats and the students began to drift away muttering Latin phrases to each other.

The senior medical lecturer mopped his brow and turned to shake Cuthbert's hand. "Thank you so much," he said. "I thought I'd lost them."

Cuthbert smiled as he said, "Oh, I know what Percy's like when he gets an audience and if we're talking about marbles, it's Percy whose lost them."

Percy still had his back to the lecture hall. He had completed his deep breath; so he raised his arms again, clenched his fists and turned … the hall was empty.

"Oh," he said.

Chapter Thirty-Seven

The journalists were no longer confined to the other block and began to mingle with the supposedly infected Valley folk. There were varied side-effects to this, as one of them bought a top-of-the-range telephoto lens from the mafia and yet another one discovered his had been swapped for a cardboard tube, covered in black felt-tip.

The reporters joined the residents at meal times and noted that the food was always eagerly awaited. Meatballs were used as squash balls, fried eggs doubled as place-mats and sausages were used to prop the windows open. No-one was sure whether anyone had actually eaten any of it yet.

Avril took on the role of head journalist/guide and was introducing everyone.

Ronald was being difficult, not just because of his secretive past, but after the bang on the head from the water cooler he couldn't remember whether his obituary said he was dead or alive.

Henry no longer seemed interested in his own past as a war reporter as to this bunch of kids he may as well have been a history teacher.

The Captain had a similar problem; every battle he mentioned his starring role in, resulted in someone checking the details on a phone and asking, "*How old are you?*" in an incredulous voice.

Elspeth was wary of these young men and women, for the truth was she had more skeletons in her closet than Cuthbert did and she also had a suspicion she herself had been young once. Some cans of worms needed to stay in the pantry.

Percy realised an audience was available and he burst into the room ready to fill the front pages of several national newspapers. Unfortunately, the hinge he tightened earlier was now so efficient it threw him back outside where the mafia pickpockets picked his wellies and he had to give chase.

Arkle wasn't available for an interview; it occurred to her since the doors had blown off and everyone was mingling, the isolation period must be pretty well over and so she went home.

Mrs Biggle appeared out of nowhere. Apparently, she spent days manning the pharmacy counter waiting for people to come and buy stamps. She tried ringing for someone to relieve her, but no one ever answered and she only left her post when her compact ran out of powder.

Cuthbert worried about his farm until someone reminded him he didn't have any animals. Then he worried about his undertaking business, until someone else reminded him the Valley had been cleared and everybody was here. Then he began to worry, because he didn't have anything to worry about.

An almighty crash and a cloud of dust interrupted the flow of questions and evasions as Percy's experimental coffee finished its sideways travel and rotted the steel cables in the shaft.

"Did anyone call for the lift?" asked the Captain.

Oliver was convinced that by moving offices he would have kept ahead of the paper trail, but already there were no corners in the room due to stacks of bills and letters addressed to patients they no longer had. At least it muffled the incessant ringing from the phone.

With the lift gone, there was only the stairs and it seemed hard work to go up to the top rooms, and so a general feeling of 'time to go home' seeped through the halls.

Belongings were collected and bumped, slid or carried down the stairs. No-one was prepared to pay the mafia's exorbitant rates for porters.

Percy shook his head in amazement. All his belongings fitted either under his hat or in his wellies, so he went to explore one last time.

It occurred to Percy that this had been rather a big adventure and no one knew of his role in saving Penelope Newgirl from a fate worse than icicles. There could be a book in this, he thought, and went in search of materials.

Oliver had negotiated a truce with Nurse Brenda, which involved a promotion and new bicycles all round, and they stood together proudly in front of the ruined hospital to announce the crisis was over.

A weary line of Valley folk stood waiting to board the buses. Their mood wasn't improved when they were told they had to wait for Percy.

Percy meanwhile went back to the x-ray department because he remembered there was a supply of paper and pens there, but this time he would avoid the machine. The shudders had only just stopped and he wasn't falling for that again; he needed a steady hand to write his book.

As he rummaged in various drawers, he found a secret stash of chocolate hidden at the back, so he put it under his hat, then he pulled a switch above him and a big light came on while he searched for more.

This searching was hard work and Percy wiped the sweat from his forehead with the back of his hand. His sweat was brown and tasty - whatever he had switched on above him had melted the chocolate, so he stuffed a supply of paper into his wellies and filled his pockets with pens before leaving.

Penelope Newgirl dutifully listened to Oliver taking all the credit for containing the plague and watched Nurse Brenda rolling her eyes as the press fired questions at them, when she spotted Percy staggering out of what was left of the isolation block.

He changed direction and headed towards them, but it wasn't the Percy she recognised from before.

Percy had been heading for the buses quite happily when he saw the press conference and decided to get some pre-publicity for his book. All the paper stuffed into his wellies made him stumble and he had to keep wiping the melting chocolate from his eyes, but he was getting nearer … when he heard a scream.

"It's a new phase!" screamed Penelope. "His face is melting," and she pointed behind Nurse Brenda.

Nurse Brenda whipped around, withdrawing a syringe from the bun of hair at the back of her head, and yelled, "Stop that man, he'll contaminate us all." The nurses ran for their bicycles.

Percy was quite used to confusion suddenly appearing before him, but it usually ran away. This time, it was coming towards him, so *he* ran.

Margery had stepped down from the bus to look for Percy, when she saw the welly-clad wally pounding towards her followed by a squadron of nurses bent over their handlebars and closing fast.

Grabbing Percy and throwing him into the bus, Margery closed the doors with a savage hiss and floored the pedal, shot-blasting the nurses with gravel before the bus gained traction and sped away.

The journalists were phoning in their headlines "Rabid Runner Runs Rings Round Authorities Again." And "Hospital running scared of the Man with the Melting Face."

Oliver watched the cloud of dust heading for the Valley taking his career with it. He would have returned to his office, but his desk was now two floors below where it had been when he left it.

Nurse Brenda yelled at two startled porters and told them to "Alert the hospital in the next town and set up an emergency Isolation Station, *right now.*"

Oliver leaned forward and removed a spare syringe from Nurse Brenda's bun and, stabbing it into her buttock, he pressed the plunger. He would *probably* catch her as she fell, he thought.

Malcolm Masters with a Masters from Maastricht watched the chaos unfold beneath him and shook his head; it certainly didn't fit into the tranquillity of the bird-watcher's world, so he decided to stay on the roof and try to fill his notebook with something other than an oddly suspicious crow.

Constable Beeching was also planning his future. He had been standing at the crossroads directing traffic for days without anyone noticing he had slipped off the bus and assumed a position of authority. He smirked, all that clever lot had been locked away and probably tortured and he had used his escape and evasion skills to hide in plain sight.

He waved another army truck on its way and turned to focus on a cloud of dust leaving the hospital.

He had lost so much weight standing here without his pizza run, if he turned too quickly, he left his uniform facing the way his body had been before he turned.

Grasping his own lapel, and heaving sideways, he rearranged everything and concentrated some of his mind on the promotion this would earn him.

The rest of his mind began to focus on the dust cloud. He narrowed his eyes - that couldn't be Margery driving, could it? If it was, she was driving very fast indeed.

Reaching for his notebook and licking his pencil took time though and, when he looked up, Margery was very close, the front of the bus was even closer and both were coming straight at him.

His last thought was, *well, at least there's a hospital nearby.*

~ The End ~

About the Author

Patrick Barrett is a sixty year old ex-miner from Mansfield in Nottinghamshire. He is married to Paula and between them, they have several children. 'Shakespeare's Cuthbert' was his first book, though he has been writing comedy for several years.

His aims as a writer are 'to be successful and make people laugh by providing them with an escape from the harshness of real life'.

His other abiding interest is in antiques.